Raising Hope

for

Darius

Suzanne,

Thank you for
your support

Sydney

Raising Hope

for

Darius

JOHNNY A. MCDOWELL

Edited by Linda Mason-Crawford
Copyedited by Mark Lorenzana
Reviewed by Janeth Parreño
Photographs by Mack T. Thornton III in association with Wanda Thompson-Brooks
and Johnny A. McDowell

Library of Congress Control Number: Pending
ISBN: Hardcover   978-1-4568-8608-0
                   Softcover   978-1-4568-8607-3
                   Ebook   978-1-4568-8609-7

TXu 1-680-108
Effective date of registration: March 19, 2010

To order additional copies of this book, contact:
Xlibris Corporation
1-888-795-4274
www.Xlibris.com
Orders@Xlibris.com
94955

CONTENTS

In loving memory of
Jacqueline Marie Harris McDowell

ACKNOWLEDGMENTS

Without God's favor upon me, none of this would be possible. I would like to thank my family for sticking by me in my darkest days. A very special thanks to my dream team, Nita Evans-Mays, Wanda Thompson-Brooks, Linda Mason-Crawford (owner of the Anchor News and Editing Services), Danise McDowell-Howard, and Mack T. Thornton III (owner of Tazzle Photography). Another very special thanks to Stephanie Watson-Swan, Sonya Gindratt-Williams, Carol Annette Johnson, Steven Shaver, Michael Green, Patrick Contreras, Sherylynn Johnson, and Michael Moncrief for all their support.

Introduction

Raising Hope for Darius is an intriguing murder mystery about two-year-old Darius, who is the only witness to the untimely death of his mother, Hope. In an attempt to cover the crime, the murderer changes his life's course, never imagining the possibility of the witness being capable of solving the case with the help of the award-winning journalist Trey who happens to be Darius' uncle.

LEFT FIELD

I felt the sting coming from my kneecaps as I settled down on the floor, and even though people were trying to lift me up, I didn't even remember falling. The moment they said my aunt was on the phone, refusing to leave a message, I knew something was terribly wrong. Neither of my aunts ever called me at school. Aunt Vera's voice seemed loud, shrieky; still, I was not prepared for the news.

"She's dead!" she said in a loud-pitched voice. "The police found her! Facedown in a pool of blood! She's dead! Oh my god, she's dead!"

Her voice, the sounds coming from the television in the media room, and the voices of people talking all around me began to restrict into a muffled sound. I felt the phone fall out of my hands and onto the floor. Whether Aunt Vera was still talking or not, hearing that Hope was dead was too much for me.

Then I saw the visions. There was my father and my mother. Suddenly I saw her—Hope—staring me dead in my face. All I wanted to do was ask them why. Why did they all have to leave me? Seeing my father staring down on me as he did when he was alive brought some deep-rooted anger back into my life for that split moment. I quickly focused on Hope because that could have been the last time I would ever see her comforting face. Though it wasn't their fault, I felt that my parents were taking the only real person that loved me unconditionally.

But why? Why would they allow my heart to be ripped from my very chest? Hope was my heart—my best friend!

An ill feeling seemed to take over my very being. My legs began to weaken, and I felt that my whole body was about to explode. This couldn't be. The vision was clear. Most definitely, it was Hope, standing there with my father and mother. A strange feeling came over me. I wanted to plead with Hope to stay with me. I wanted to reach out and talk some sense into her. How could this be? What, where, when, and how could anyone take such a beautiful person from this earth?

Were the tears falling from my eyes interfering with my vision? Were they leaving me? I begged Hope not to leave me!

I was totally dysfunctional, incoherent for a better word because reasoning was zero! My world was in chaos.

Nobody in this world could make me believe that my best friend in the whole wide world died of a heroin overdose. Aunt Vera said she went to the house, and even though Hope refused to answer the door, she could hear Darius crying his heart out. Finally, she called the police from the neighbor's house next door.

Once the police arrived, they tried getting Hope to respond to the numerous requests to open the door, and after several requests, they kicked the door in and found her lying in a pool of blood, a belt tied around her arm, a syringe in her arm, and Darius covered in blood from head to toe.

Aunt Vera was not allowed to hold Darius or take him home with her. She followed the ambulance that took Darius to Hillcrest Hospital in hopes of getting him, but that wasn't about to happen.

The last call I made to Aunt Vera from the airport before boarding my flight to Dallas closed the door on what I already knew was going to happen to Darius. He was turned over to Child Protective Services, and the only way I was going to be able to get him back was by order of a judge.

My flight was finally in the air and headed to Dallas. I sat there in my seat, looking at the powder blue space, trying to figure out why Hope would do such a thing or allow such a thing to happen to her. Suicide, a drug overdose? The whole scene was too far-fetched for anyone to believe when it came to Hope, and I was no different. This was not Hope's doing. She loved Darius. She loved me. She didn't do this.

One thing was for sure, I wasn't returning to my life in Atlanta any time soon, and I wasn't leaving Waco until I found out the truth about Hope.

I sat on the plane and did something I hadn't done in years. I prayed. I asked God to turn over the truth to the investigating officers so that whoever did this to my sister would be caught by the time I got to Waco. God did show me some mercy because sleep found me as I drifted off thinking about my mom and dad and Hope.

(The past kept creeping into my head.) It was right after my father died—six months to be exact, and between him not being in my mother's life anymore and us running down my selfish sister—it was hard to tell why Mama cried so much and who was hurting her the most. I thought Mama's crying would at least ease up after a while, but two months into my father's death, Hope started running the streets as if her freedom was part of Emancipation Proclamation at the expense of Daddy's death.

I remember staring into the television screen with a conscious intent, surrounded by all of Hope's accomplishments, and subconsciously, I asked myself why she was doing what she was doing. From the time she could speak, Mama had her in all types of pageants and modeling for Dillard's and JCPenney's store advertisement. When it came to my father, she was taking up Tae Kwon Do, and between the modeling and state tournaments in martial arts, awards, ribbons, medals, newspaper articles, the trophies just kept coming and coming.

It was evident that my parents were nose to nose about who loved Hope the most, and with all the attention that she was receiving from the both of them, she had things her way. Sometimes things between Mama and Daddy got pretty heated because of Hope, and though I was envious, I stayed out of the way and buried myself into my schoolwork. I made the honor roll from the seventh grade and didn't stop until I graduated from high school and still didn't receive what Hope was receiving from our parents.

One thing I can honestly say about my sister, though, I was her best friend, and she gave me half the world that was given to her. Nevertheless, I found myself sitting there at one end of the house at two thirty in the morning. I'm wondering where the hell Hope was, what she was doing at this time of the night, and why were things so far in left field for us all.

I had heard Mama tell my aunt Jean that Hope was grown now, but for me, though, she was nineteen. That wasn't an excuse to have Mama crying every day. If I even knew that I could whip her, I would track her down and wherever I found her is where she would get her ass torn off the bone! But since I was no fool, it was safer for me to just wait up like Mama was doing and hope that she came home in one piece. Hope didn't have what I would consider a best friend, so I couldn't really just call somebody to inquire about where, what, when, or if they had seen her.

Word around town was Hope was hanging out with this known pimp named Spoon, but such a rumor was hard to believe, especially concerning Hope. Other than a few boys from the church who braved to handle her beauty and her not accepting any bullshit, I never knew of her having a steady boyfriend, but a pimp? This I definitely couldn't believe.

It was right about four o'clock when I heard the garage door open, and I was storming toward her, only to be stopped by my mother. "Trey, leave her be," she said as she withdrew back into her room and closed her door.

"She's not the one that has to sit here and listen to you crying every day because of her crap, Mama," I reminded her of that fact, but she just closed her door. I stormed out to the garage anyway. I couldn't allow Hope to set foot inside the house because if I did, I couldn't talk my shit in the manner that I wanted to without disrespecting Mama.

I was lucky enough to catch her placing something in the trunk of her car, and I quietly closed the door behind me, just enough to get her attention.

"Why do we have to keep going through this same stuff night after night, Hope?"

"Why don't you just stop tryin' to be my daddy and get you some business, Trey?"

"That's just it, if Daddy was still living, you wouldn't be taking Mama through this bullshit."

Hope shut her trunk and started walking past me without answering me. I shoved her back up against her car. "Don't do that again, Trey!"

"Or what, Hope? You gonna kick my ass?" I asked, walking within inches of her. "You got Mama crying every day behind your selfishness. What has she done to deserve this shit from you?"

"Trey, I'm going to ask you one time to move out of my way."

"If you raise a hand at me, we gone mess each other up, and I mean it," I said as I stood face-to-face with her.

"Boy, I'm grown and I can come and go as I please."

"If you're that grown, move your ass out of this house so that you can take your selfish foot off of Mama's neck."

She brushed past me and said, "Believe me, I'm workin' on that."

I grabbed her by the back of her blouse and pulled her back to me. "You haven't answered my question yet!"

She reacted with a dislodging technique to separate herself from me. "I'm tired of doing and being what other people want me to be, Trey. I'm not happy about Daddy dying, and I'm not punishing Mama either, Trey," she said with tears in her eyes.

"You could have fooled me," I said.

"Is Mama asleep?" she asked.

"What do you think, Hope? And what's up with this pimp dude you're supposed to be kickin' it with?"

"His name is Spoon, and for the record, I'm not a hoe and nor do I plan to become one either. So I wish you and everybody else would give me more credit than that, for God's sake."

"Hope, it's four thirty in the morning this time, so how much credit should a crying mother extend to your ass? Please tell me."

"Does she know?" asked Hope.

"Everybody knows. Hell, it's not like you give a damn either."

"I'm moving in with him."

"Oh, like that's going to ease Mama's mind, Hope! So to hell with college and your future, huh?"

"I'm thinking about all of that right now for your information, Trey."

"Yeah, save that for the rest of Spoon's hoes," I said as I walked past her.

"So you hate me now?" she asked. Her question stopped me in my tracks.

"I've missed out on a semester of college because of how you've started to handle Mama. Surely you didn't think that I was just going to leave her here under the love you're trying to serve her up with? So in case you hadn't gotten the word yet, I'm staying home and have enrolled at Paul Quinn so that I can take care of our mother. Everything has always been about Hope, and I guess there ain't no end to it, is it?" I asked, but instead of waiting for her answer, I walked off toward my bedroom.

Another six months passed, and though I had a room on the campus, Mama's welfare was more important than living the college life. Hope's bullshit rose to an all-time high. It was months before she would come by the house or weeks before she would even call Mama.

Mama got to the point that she would ask me to find Hope, see if she was okay, and inform her so that she could find some peace in knowing that Hope was alright. I saw her at the 7-Eleven convenience store one morning with a fresh dressing wrapped around her forearm, and she told me that she got into it with one of Spoon's ex-hoes. Come to find out, Hope regulated with two of Spoon's hoes to let them know that she was the overseer of Spoon's affairs.

Even though Hope and Spoon lived away from his den, Hope was still used as a "get right bitch," and from what I knew of my sister, if Spoon got out of line, he would have to shoot her because she wouldn't hesitate to bust him in half or place him in the emergency room. So he used her to keep his girls in line.

Another time, Mama and I were just leaving church, and like most Sundays, I took her to the Piccadilly Cafeteria out on the Lake Air Mall for dinner. By the time I found a parking spot and got around to Mama's side of the car to open her door, Hope and Spoon walked out of the mall and saw us.

This was Mama's first time seeing Spoon, and it had been two months since she had laid eyes on Hope. We all froze in our tracks for about five seconds. Hope broke the ice by walking toward us with Spoon in tow.

"Mama, this is Spoon." Hope looked into Mama's eyes. Mama looked Spoon up and down and then looked back to Hope. Without warning, Mama lifted her hand as if she was about to say hi to somebody. Instead, she slapped Hope in the face as hard as she could.

"Don't you ever disgrace me another day in your life!" Mama told Hope. Then she got back in the car and slammed the door.

"You know she comes here on Sundays, Hope," I said as I walked back around to the other side of the car.

"I'm sorry, Mama," Hope shouted through the window, but Mama continued to look straight ahead without acknowledging her.

I asked Mama if she was okay. "My daughter just disrespected me and violated my space with that nothing, but I'll be all right. How dare she tread on my water like that!"

I asked her where she wanted to go now, and she replied, "Just take me home, baby."

After that day, it was like Waco, Texas, got smaller because the four of us couldn't walk across the street without seeing one another. I could never tell where Mama's head and heart were because the crying stopped. As a replacement, she became emotionless about Hope.

The holidays came and went with a small dinner for two and was never compromised with even a thought of Hope showing up. If or whenever Hope did call or drop by, Mama never mentioned it for whatever reason; instead, she stored it in her heart.

Shortly after, I felt a hard change about to come over me and my mother because Paul Quinn was about to close its doors in Waco and was moving students and staff to Dallas.

For Mama, there was no consideration about my stopping classes. I was to go to Dallas for my final year, and graduate. With the week of my departure coming up, I found a need to locate Hope to inform her of my leaving town and to see if she would take some time to check on Mama.

I had never visited Hope's numerous homesteads, so I had to pass through the hoe strolls to drop word for her to call me or to tell Spoon to have her call me. It was midafternoon when I spotted Spoon parked on the stroll, talking to one of his girls. As soon as he spotted my car pulling up, he motioned for the girl to leave.

"This ain't a politically correct spot for you to travel down, Trey, so I know if you're down here, it's important."

"I need to speak with Hope."

"You talkin' as if you askin' for permission to do that, and I want you to know that it's not ever like that, youngsta. Get in your car and follow me," he stated.

I followed him out to Lake Shore Drive and pulled into the driveway of a nice brick house with a yard that was kept far better than my mother's. As I got out of my car, he rolled down his window. "I'll let the two of you talk in peace. Just ring the doorbell, and, Trey, you're welcomed to stop by anytime you get ready. If Hope ever knew you were on the cuts lookin' for her, she would have a fit."

"Damn, brother, man, I'm touched by that," I said with a serious look on my face.

"Have it your way. Your way, youngsta," he said before backing out of the driveway. I guess Hope heard the car door slam and decided to look out the window because she was standing in the doorway when I turned around.

"What's wrong, Trey?"

"I'm leaving town, that's what's wrong!" I said as she stood back for me to walk through the door of her home. I had to admit, her taste wasn't too far off from her upbringing, and from the looks of things, she had Spoon spending a lot of money.

"I heard Quinn was closing, but didn't know it was this soon. So you're going to Dallas, huh?"

"Can you take some time out of your busy schedule to check on Mama every day, Hope?"

"Mama doesn't want me callin' or stoppin' by that much, Trey."

"Matters that, Hope! Besides, how is she supposed to feel about her daughter?"

"Trey, it's been over three years now," she said as she walked into the kitchen.

I followed her, continuing, "I'm not here to discuss issues between the two of you or be a mediator either. You checkin' on Mama or not, girl?"

"Boy, you know I am, so stop trippin'!" she said, then handed me a cold glass of beer.

"All this shit paid for?" I asked.

"Trey, the man peddles hoes for a living. How much credit do you expect him to have?"

"I guess you still thinking about college?" I asked her as I drank from my glass.

"Please don't start, Trey."

"Just asking!"

"So where are you going, and what are you going to do after graduation?"

"I'm pursuing journalism."

"Get off the bullshit, you?" she said with a smile on her face. That was the first time that I felt my sister's presence since our father passed away, and instead of embarrassing her, all I wanted to know was, why this life?

"I enjoy what they do, and though it's far from the articles I write about on and off campus, that's what I want to do."

"I'm proud of you, Trey." I hadn't hugged Hope since the afternoon of Daddy's funeral, and I took the opportunity to do just that. Neither of us wanted to let go. She had been yearning for some family love, and I missed my best friend.

"Don't be mad at me, Trey," she whispered.

"I'm learning not to be, Hope," I said as I released her.

"You coming home on the weekends?" she asked.

"If I don't, Mama will trip, and I really don't want to add to her burdens."

"So is that what I am?" she asked.

"Naw, Hope! Mama has medical issues, girl. Bad heart, high blood pressure, and borderline diabetic to top that."

"Don't worry about Mama. I got her, and thank you for tellin' me."

"Please don't tell her I said anything about this because she'll be mad at me," I said as I walked toward the front door.

"Why are you so in a rush to leave?" she asked.

I told her that I had some unfinished business to tend to before I pulled out. As I backed out of the driveway, I had to let Hope know how I felt about her. "I love you, Hope!"

"I love you too, Trey." She started crying.

By the time I walked through the house door, Mama was standing in the doorway of her bedroom, looking my way. "How is she doing?" she asked.

"She's doing all right Mama, and how did you know I went to see her?"

"I'm a mother, Trey!"

"She's coming by, so get ready."

"You also told her about my health too," she declared.

"Matters what lies between us, Mama. She needed to know."

"I don't need her coming by here out of sympathy."

"Mama, please stop it! The girl loves you more than you'll ever know, so just stop it. Please!" She shook her head and turned away, indicating that our conversation was over.

Mama felt the need to spoil me with some shopping every day until I left. Our departure from each other wasn't an emotional one because she knew I was just up the highway and would be back home in a few weeks. With the college going through a resettling, things were going to be hectic on the student body and administration as well.

I bought Hope a pair of diamond earrings and went by her crib to give them to her the day I left, but she wasn't home. So I left them in her mailbox with a short letter.

By the time I made it on campus of the old Bishop College, I had a note on my dorm door, asking me to come down to the front desk. When I finally got down there, I was handed an envelope. Hope had called to thank me for the earrings and, on the cool, to let me know she was keeping up with her little brother.

FOR MAMA

Spring break conversations were being tossed up as if this was the last opportunity to find some reward for the hard work we all had put in toward the closing of the previous semester. I, on the other hand, had only plans to start packing all my stuff to avoid the congested exodus come May.

Graduation was coming up, but for me, my objectives of becoming a journalist needed just another stop, and I had to go to Atlanta for that. You would have thought the student body learned a thing or two about having to pack up and move from the Waco-to-Dallas experience, but to each their own!

My grades were so good that I met with the president of the college about the possibility of taking my exams a month early so that I could start making my way toward the campus of Clark University in Georgia. All my professors were contacted on the matter, and all but one had yet to make up his exam, so I had to wait until the first week of April.

It was only Wednesday, and as badly as I wanted to ditch my Thursday classes to get some extra time away from such a congested environment, I was only headed back to Waco and not a vacation spot, so I chilled.

Mama was really surprised about my choice to go to Atlanta because that would take me farther away from her, and I had turned into what she considered a Mama's boy. I made it a point to tell her how disappointed Daddy would be if I didn't take care of her the way that I do.

On the cool, though, with all the grief she was going through behind my father's death and her princess turning her back on her, all she needed was for me to end up doing something crazy. That would have pushed her over the edge. Nevertheless, I was surprised that she had hung on through her heartaches as long as she did.

It was three forty-five Thursday morning when our dorm monitor came knocking at my door to inform me that my mother was in the hospital. Doctor didn't expect her to make it through the day.

It was now six that same morning when I walked through the doors of Hillcrest Hospital. Right today I wholeheartedly believe that God escorted me straight to my mother and gave me just enough time to speak with her before taking her soul.

As I approached the elevators to take me up to the seventh floor, all eight elevator doors stood wide open for me, waiting to take me to my mother. As I walked toward her room, I knew that time was limited, and she was doing all she could to hold on just to see me.

"My baby," she uttered in a calm and relieved voice.

"Mama, you have to pull through this for me. Please, Mama."

"Don't you go getting all teary eyed on me right now, baby. I'm so proud of you, Trey. You have been such a wonderful son. I need for you to pick your head up and not allow my passing to be hard on you. You've always carried around so much baggage, Trey. Yeah, you didn't think I knew, huh? I'm your mother, baby. Your father loved you very much."

"Mama, don't go. Please. Not now."

"Your father's here, Trey. Watch out for your sister. She made me a promise, Trey. You see that she honors her word. Can you do that for Mama?"

"I got you, Mama. I got you!" I kissed her check and took a deep breath to preserve her scent in my soul.

"I love you, Trey." Those were her last words, and then, she was gone.

An hour passed, and I was still at Mama's side, holding her hand and caressing her face. Hope and the hospital staff interrupted my thoughts.

"Trey, let her go, baby. She's gone, and we have to let these people do what they do," Hope said.

"What did you promise Mama, Hope?" I asked as I continued to stroke Mama's face.

"Trey . . ."

"What was it, Hope?" I stopped her, looking into her face with a cold stare.

"I promised her that I would get back into church and stop living how I'm living."

"Don't make Mama wait too long, and if you dishonor Mama, you dishonor me. Are we clear on this?" My sister and I looked deeply, face-to-face. "I'm not going to leave her hangin', Trey," she stated as she wiped the tears from my face.

Hope and I stood outside of my mother's hospital room until they brought her body out. With all that just happened, the legalities concerning Mama's body never crossed my mind. Hope told me that she would take care of Mama's funeral if I didn't mind.

"I don't want Spoon at her funeral, and make sure you don't leave Mama's purse or any of her belongings when you leave this place. I'll be at the house," I said before walking off.

As I left the hospital, I could only think about mine and Mama's discussion and how she revealed what was in my heart concerning my father. All my life, I thought I had been doing a good job at hiding what I felt about him. From the time I was seven or eight, I started counting the times my father would tell me he loved me like he told Hope, and that only ended up being nine times.

With Mama knowing such a thing, I wondered if the two of them ever talked about the issue when he was alive. I guess it really didn't matter anymore. Outside of my two aunts and some distant cousins that I had only seen twice in my life, it was just me and Hope left.

The way she had tripped out in the past, I really questioned whether or not she was going to honor her word to Mama. Despite her treating Mama the way that she did, Mama still loved her and couldn't see not leaving Hope something.

One thing Mama did years ago was place me over her finances and made me promise to give Hope half of whatever money was left but only if she got away from Spoon. She said she wouldn't rest knowing that a pimp was living off her money. Mama also left me the house because she wasn't about to leave it with Hope. Whatever Mama and Hope talked about before I arrived, they both had time to vent. It was weird pulling up to the house and not seeing Mama lift one of the mini blinds to see which one of us was coming home.

By the time I let my garage door back down and walked into the house through the kitchen entryway, I knew I was not alone in the house. Both Mama and Daddy's aura was so thick that it was uncomfortable to me. As I looked at the calendar hanging from the refrigerator by a round magnet on a hook, I counted the days before exam time.

I realized I had a lot to do and not enough time to think about how I was going to get it done. I made up my mind right there and then that I would pay up the utilities for a year, with the exception of the phone, and get Hope to check on the house. I couldn't see turning everything off and moving out when I only had a little over a year to go in school. At least I could come back home for the holidays.

It wasn't a question that Mama would want my aunts to have her clothes, shoes, and hats—but her jewelry . . . now that would be over Hope's dead body! Outside of those things, I didn't see anything else leaving out of the house.

Two hours passed, and I heard one of the garage doors open and then close. Minutes later, Hope came walking through the kitchen with some of Mama's belongings. She handed me Mama's purse. I reached out slowly to take it because I didn't know what she expected me to do with it. Hope sensed my confusion and said, "Mama's life is in the purse and since you're over everything, you'll need what's in it."

"How did Mama get to the hospital?" I asked.

"That's a silly question, Trey! I took her. So if you're looking for a reason to start in on me, forget it! I told you when you left my house that I would look after her, and I did. So back off!"

"I'm sorry," I said.

"Don't worry about it. What are you going to do about this house?" she asked.

"I'm paying the utilities up for a year, and I'll deal with it when I get back. If you want the phone left on, you pay for it, and if not, I'm having it cut off."

"You better get Mama's jewelry and whatever you don't want Aunt Vera and Aunt Jean to have because they're coming. I'm not giving them anything else, so don't let them talk you into letting them back in here while I'm in Atlanta."

"I'm going to need to come home when I move out of my situation," Hope stated. She waited for me to respond, but before I could even say her name, she continued. "I won't have anywhere else to go, Trey. On top of that, I'm going back to school, and the money I have saved up, I'm using it to live on while I'm in school. I won't let him set foot in this house, so don't go there."

"So when is all this going to take place?" I asked.

"Damn, can we get Mama in the ground first, Trey?" she shouted. We both sat in silence for more than twenty minutes.

"Is Spoon gonna trip about you leaving?"

"I run me, Trey!"

"You're all I have left, if I even feel like some shit is wrong, I'm movin' in on the fool!"

"Stop thinking crazy, Trey!"

"I've been looking for a reason to beat his sweet ass up anyway."

"I wish you wouldn't get in my business and let me do this my way. When are you supposed to be in Atlanta anyway?"

"By the end of May."

"Hell, you sitting here worried about my business, and you're fighting for more time your damn self."

"Forget all of that. Have you made funeral arrangements?" I asked.

"It's scheduled for Monday at eleven. She already told me what she wanted to wear, so I have to go shopping."

"I'm going to need you to hang out with me Monday and Tuesday so that we can get this legal stuff out of the way."

"You just hold yourself together, and let's get past this funeral," she said as she kissed me on the forehead and then left the house.

The days leading up to Mama's funeral were more of an invasion of Hope's and my privacy and everybody trying to take something from my mother's house, but I was stiff about saying *no*! I won't sit here and say that Mama's funeral went well because it was the hardest thing I've ever had to do, but I was glad that it was over.

After Hope and I made our rounds to finish tying up loose ends, Mama ended up having a soft heart for Hope anyway. She left us every dime Daddy left her, and after it was said and done, I ended up with $150,000, the house, and some land. Hope ended up with $60,000 and a CD worth $15,000.

After we both found out that we had a nice piece of change, she wouldn't let me pay up the utilities like I said I was going to do. We did lunch together and went to visit our parents' graves before I left the city.

It wasn't until May 20 that I returned back to Waco, and my first stop was my parents' grave sites. I hadn't spoken to Hope all but two times in almost two months. But by the looks of fresh flowers on their graves, Hope was being mindful.

As I walked toward the house, Hope was out front watering the lawn and every part of the landscaping was the way Mama and Daddy would have had it.

I don't know if it was because of not being dragged around doing shit for Spoon all day or a sign of good living, but Hope had put on a few pounds and was looking like the sister I grew up with. As I drove up into the driveway, she started spraying down my car with water, refusing to let me out of my car. So I crawled over to my passenger side before she could get to that side and got out.

"Playful these days, huh?" I asked her. "One smart word, boy, and I'll hose your ass down like a fire," she playfully said.

"Damn, don't I get a 'hey little brother,' a hug, kiss, some type of greeting?"

"Oh, I'm sorry. Here you go!" she said, and she began to hose me down.

Athletically inclined as she was, running up on her was a waste of time, so I went for a section of the hose, bent a crease into it, and cut the water flow off. After the water finished covering my eyesight, I saw Hope for who she really was, and I froze.

"Hope, you're pregnant!"

"So what else is new, Dr. Allen? I was that before you left."

"How come you didn't say anything?" I asked.

"Too much was going on already," she replied. "So did Mama know?" I asked. "Yeah! In fact, she gave me a girl's name if it's a girl and a boy's for if it's a boy. Having an abortion was out of the picture for the both of us. So to ease her mind, I agreed to leave Spoon. I didn't and she sure didn't want her grandson being associated with a pimp."

I asked her if Spoon knew, and she told me not yet.

"What do you mean 'not yet'?"

"I haven't made up my mind yet, Trey."

"Are you still seeing him?" I asked, releasing the water hose, walking up to her, and kissing her cheek.

"I've seen him twice, and I talk to him at least once a day."

"Damn, you don't have that much time left to be thinking," I said as I felt the growth of her stomach.

"He thinks that I'm seeing someone else, and so do Aunt Jean and Aunt Vera."

"I guess news has traveled like electricity between those two," I stated.

"Boy, you don't know the half of it. I sit with them at church, and they sit up like proud den mothers. Boy, why are you still rubbing on my stomach?"

"I had to make sure that it was a boy."

"And how would you know something like that?" she asked.

"You didn't know? I'm the shit, girl!"

"Boy, shut your crazy ass up."

"Put a grand on it!" I said, sticking my hand out for a bet shake.

"That's a bet, and I want my money too," she said as we shook hands.

"So what did Mama name him?" I asked.

"She said Darius and spelled it out so that I could get it right. She said that she had been holding on to that name since I was fifteen."

"Damn! Mama had you pregnant before your time, girl." We both laughed.

"Don't you want to know what the girl's name is?"

"Unless my skills are off, and I doubt that you're having twins, put her on the back burner because Darius is on the way."

"Put that hose up and come clean up so that I can take your fat ass to dinner." I teased her and then had to run into the house to avoid getting hosed down again.

"Oh, you've really pissed me off now," she said as she did her best to get me.

When I got into the house, my subconscious did an overview scan for the presence of my mother, and though Hope was putting her flavor in the decor, Mama was still running the show.

I heard two taps of a car horn and immediately assumed it was Spoon. I wasn't too quick to find me a shadowed spot to conceal myself so I could get my nosy on, so I just went to the front door and found out who the visitor was.

She was pretty much known to me and a lot of other brothers as a wasted good woman!

Though her name was Ms. Katrina Bibles, she was also known as Kat in the streets and one of the finest women a brother ever laid eyes on. Sad thing about the sister, her ethics, morals, and principles had a five-minute time limit on her profession as a street hoe, and she was flat backin' for Spoon.

I got around to asking her why she was doing the things that she was doing, and her only response was "Some hoes are nurses, doctors, teachers, business owners, and factory workers, but one thing that we all have in common. We all fuckin' for a cause. I just choose not to be discreet about mine."

Kat had tried to take Hope out from under Spoon's grasp so that she wouldn't fall prey to the street life of a hoe but come to find out it was Spoon who actually got turned out and almost cost him his stable, Kat explained. So Hope took on the role as Spoon's bottom hoe just to keep his girls from running off.

Through it all, Kat and Hope ended up being friends. Despite Kat's obligations to Spoon, her loyalty was always with Hope. Now that Hope was out of the way, Kat took over as Spoon's bottom hoe and was most likely living under the same roof with him while the other girls lived together in another house on the opposite side of the tracks.

It was clear that Kat knew Hope was pregnant because the first thing Kat did when she got out of her car was feel on Hope's stomach. Obviously, her loyalty was still on Hope's end.

I walked out the front door to get all my belongings that I brought home from Quinn and knew that I was going to be put on blast as soon as Kat saw me. I guess my metamorphosis from a high school geek to a prime USDA piece of meat kept her wet. The last time I saw her, she offered me twenty-two hundred dollars for an hour, but I couldn't see myself pushing up on her.

"Ooooh my baby's home," Kat stated as she trotted over to wrap her arms around me. For me, giving her a peck on her cheek was out of the question, and her putting her lips on me was damn sure out of the question, and she respected the game like that.

"How are things with you, Kat?"

"Trey, you know what it is, but one thing for sure, if Kat can make it better for Kat, that's what it is!"

"So why don't you just get out then?" I asked.

"Baby, as sure as there is a god in heaven, if you asked me to and wanted me as your girl, I would spoil your ass with the best life had to offer. If it took me to sell every square inch of 5 foot 6, 165 pounds of this 34, 21, 38, the world would be yours, daddy."

"But what about what you want, Kat?" I asked as I pushed her curly locked hair back in place.

"Trey, that's what I do, baby."

"So how do you think Spoon is going to feel knowing his main girl is ready to jump ship for me?"

"A pimp respects every aspect of the game, and, daddy, if you got enough to pull his bottom hoe, nigga, you can have his whole stable."

"Thanks for the education, boo, but I'll stick with my day job."

Kat asked me about school. I was ready to end this conversation, but I answered, "It's demanding at times and then again I get my row out when I feel the need. Listen, I don't mean to be rude, but can I get you to limit your conversation with Ms. Thang so that she can come clean up? We're supposed to be having dinner, and I'm hungry." I pointed to Hope, hoping she would back me up.

"Five minutes, daddy, and she's yours," she said.

I gave Kat another hug to feel the firmness of her body up against mine, and she whispered into my ear. "I ain't ever been too proud to beg for what I want. I've got $5,000, Trey. Can I have you for an hour, please?"

"I can't, Kat," I said, releasing her.

"Take care of yourself, Kat. And, Hope, wrap this up so that we can move around, girl."

"Boy, I'm coming," she said with a smile on her face. Hope knew that Kat was trying to push up on me and knew that I wasn't going to bite Kat's bait.

After I unloaded my car, I saw a few boxes of things that belonged to Mama, and it was evident that Hope wasn't giving them up. I noticed that Hope moved into Mama's bedroom, and as big as the house was,

I wouldn't want to be alone in the house unless I was right in the center of it.

It took Hope two hours to find something to wear and at least thirty-five "how does this look, Trey" before she settled for the first piece she had put on.

We found ourselves at the Red Lobster but only after stopping at several places on Valley Mills Drive that we couldn't get into because the smell of the food was making Hope nauseated. "Girl, we've wasted a half tank of gas behind your keen and sensitive sensors. Don't get me in here, and you conclude that seafood is not what you want."

"Trey, get your butt out of the car, and let's go eat."

It had been awhile since I had some good seafood, and I ordered enough food for myself to feed two people. Hope, on the other hand, was totally out of control. She ordered up shit just to take a few bites of the dish and kept ordering. Crazy ass girl's bill was $140 but she was content after her feed.

She sat back away from the table and looked at me. "So are you ready for Atlanta?" I'm ready to establish myself as a journalist."

"So you really going eighteen hours away from home to learn how to be nosy and stay into somebody's business? Hell, you could get Aunt Vera and Aunt Jean to teach you how to do that and save yourself a lot of money."

"Hope, that ain't funny, girl!"

"Darius will be here in about six and a half months, and I need you home for at least a week. I don't think I could take Vera and Jean at the house for two weeks, not to mention the first week after I deliver this boy."

"Aaah, you've accepted the fact that it's a boy, huh?"

"Only because that's what you want," she said as she tossed a piece of bread at me.

"Call me when you start going into labor, and I'll catch the next flight out to Dallas, and I'll drive here from there, so don't trip."

"If you give me a week to rest and keep Vera and Jean at bay, I'll be mentally ready to deal with them after that."

"So how do you plan to deal with Spoon, concerning your child?"

"Oh, so it's *child* now!"

"Hope, stop playing, girl. I'm serious."

"To be honest with you, Trey, I've been trying to talk him out of the streets. Outside of what he does for a living, he's really a good brother."

"Is this a campaign stance for something that you're about to do, Hope?"

"Shit, your nosy skills are already up to par!" she stated. "Yes or no?" I asked.

"I want Darius to have a father, Trey, and if that means getting Spoon to stop his street hustling and do something respectable for a living, then I'll be satisfied."

"Hope, if the man doesn't know he has a child on the way, what other options does he have or that you can say to him that will be a consideration to leave the streets? Hell, even Kat's mentality is screwed up! This shit is crazy."

"If he won't do it for God—"

I had to interrupt her with that. "God! The man is a pimp, Hope. Pussy equals money, and getting baptized or doing communion ain't in the scope of pimpin'."

"I at least got him to where he's thinkin' about it. He's been to jail twice in the past, and the Feds really want to turn the girls against him to get him behind bars, but they're standing true to him."

"I can see it now. Spoon being baptized, and the water starts to boil."

"Trey, shut your crazy ass up. You kill me with your skepticism about something you don't understand anyway."

"Put another grand on him stayin' at his current occupation or flippin' pussy at 'Tricks and Chumps.' I'm not bettin' on anything like that, plus, God might turn him while you playin'."

"I can tell you're back in church," I stated.

"You act as if that's a bad thing, silly ass boy."

"For you, girl, hallelujah, praise God, thank you, Jesus!" I said as I got up in the restaurant and did my rendition of a holy dance.

"Trey, sit your crazy ass down, fool," she said as she laughed, along with all the customers around us.

I slid in next to her and kissed her on the cheek.

"Stupid, just stupid, Trey."

"Thank you for doing right by Mama, Hope. I know she's watching you with frowns on her face behind you trying to get Spoon in church."

"Well, don't count the Man upstairs out too soon, Mr. Know-it-all!"

"Girl, let's get out of this place. I'm full and sleepy." I had already started yawning.

"Yeah, you need to hurry up and move because I'm fartin' my ass off, and I want some ice cream before I go to sleep."

"Damn, Hope!" I said as I fanned her funk. "You bring your stinkin' ass out in the parking lot, and don't be doing that shit in my car."

"Trey, stop trippin' because it's not me, it's your nephew."

"The boy don't even have an asshole yet, Hope, so bring your stinkin' ass on," I said as I helped her up from the table.

We were doing the sibling thing so well that I didn't want to ruin the date by telling her I would be staying in Atlanta for an extended eighteen months. I had been hired to work as an intern for one of Atlanta's newspapers. Things looked like they were going well, and that made me even more comfortable about accomplishing my objectives without worrying about Hope, the house, or my up-and-coming nephew.

By the time we returned to the house, Spoon's car was parked out front; and by the frowns on her face, Hope was unsettled about his being there. "Trey, go in the house," she told me, making eye contact to let me know she could handle Spoon.

He looked toward us and pleaded, "Hope, don't trip, and I know you don't like me invading your space, but I want to talk if it's all right with you."

I gave Spoon the normal heads-up we black men usually give each other in our nonverbal communication, and he returned it. At that moment, I saw the submissive side of Spoon and knew right then that he was sprung on Hope. I looked back at Hope before I took another step.

"Trey, it's cool," she said, and I went in the house.

Whatever it was that brought him over was enough to risk Hope going off. The only mean streak I've ever known her to have was against this opponent of hers out of Killeen, Texas. Hope had led in the scoring at a state competition the first two rounds, but at the end of the third, the judges ruled the girl the winner by a point.

Hope stalked this girl through the newspaper article that hung in her room, her bathroom, the inside of her locker at school, at the gym, and in her history book. A whole year came full circle, and when Hope faced her again, she punished her something serious and stared at the judges after every round. She never returned to competition fighting again.

So for him to brave Hope's mean streak, he came with the right attitude and demeanor. Hope didn't come into the house for three hours, and whatever they talked about, Hope was winning, and it showed on her face. I didn't inquire about the meeting the whole time I was at the house. I knew whatever she was up to was going to eventually come to a head.

Downfall

A year and a half later

I hadn't been home since Darius had started crawling, and though I only reserved my opportunities to make it home due to my hectic schedule, I wasn't prepared for what was waiting for me back in Waco on this trip.

What could have gone so damn wrong, Hope, when things were going so right? I was still sitting on the runway in Atlanta for a whole forty-five minutes behind schedule because two emergency landings were requested from two incoming flights, and so all outgoing flights were halted.

All I could think about was Darius and started reminiscing. He had Hope in labor for nine hours. He would bring on the indications that he was coming and then change his mind. Nevertheless, he gave me ample time to catch a flight out of Atlanta, drive into Waco, and within the next hour or two, Hope's water broke.

I felt like a proud father as the nurse handed him to me, and from the looks of his struggles, the youngster was ready to get some sleep and so was Hope. I had taken off for two weeks because Hope was trying to get a breath of fresh air, and that was totally impossible with Aunt Jean and Aunt Vera around.

I felt as if I was forced into fatherhood because all Hope did for a whole week was sleep, and I took care of the rest. I made some guidelines for Kat to follow when it came down to Darius. *No perfume, fresh clothes, six hours without tricking, and no touching.* I wasn't about to let her world come into contact with him under any circumstances.

Donald Simms, a.k.a. Spoon, had gained some respect with me because he left the streets and was very active in the church. I had questioned whether his abrupt switch was due to possible federal charges for taking his show across state lines or Hope's mojo. But either way, I allowed him to visit without restrictions.

Hope decided not to tell Donald that Darius was his son because he was still showing some signs that he was still holding on to a portion of the street life. I was in no kind of position to dispute her knowledge or instinct because I was too square when it came to shit like that.

Deep down inside, Donald knew Darius was his, but he respected the game enough to take a backseat to Hope's wishes and on the cool, him having or showing love to anyone outside of himself was something that wasn't present within him or taught in Pimpin' 101.

As time went on, Darius grew, Hope was glued to the church and had enrolled into McLennan Community College to pursue her beginning stages of a counseling degree, and Donald moved up the ranks in the church from having a young men's mentoring group to teaching a Sunday school class to becoming a deacon and, within fifteen months, was now known as Reverend Simms.

Though he was only the assistant pastor at Mt. Zion Hill Baptist Church, his style of preaching packed the pews, and when he was invited to preach at other churches, he would only accept the invitation if the church was large enough to hold his church members too because they followed Donald wherever he went.

The more comfortable I had gotten about Hope maintaining without me being around, the more I dug deeper into my objective of becoming a journalist. When I started my internship, I was looking forward to being given at least half the chance to showcase my desire, but instead, I had become more of a scientific experiment gone bad.

After six and a half months, I woke up looking in the mirror and seeing myself as part gofer, part mule, and part ass who had forgotten what I came to Atlanta for. I literally had to almost get fired by refusing to comply with the orders and demands of my supervisors.

It was either you give me an assignment or you fire me, and at that time, I didn't give a damn. If it was to find out why a dog's shit fell the direction it did, I wanted it! I was told to report to the assignment supervisor's office in two hours. At the time, every reporter in Atlanta was concentrating on the Atlanta murders or trying to be the first to expose this person.

I couldn't bring myself to think about nothing shorter than my own piece of the pie, and this was going to be my chance to prove myself. The two hours were up, and my orders were to interview the Atlanta Independent School District's superintendent and the principals at all the high school and junior high schools to find out why the students were having two separate proms at a time when segregation was no longer allowed.

Whether or not my story was going to catch the eyes of a reader or not, whites and African-Americans having separate proms was a shocker to me, and being that it wasn't a close-kept secret to the city of Atlanta, I wanted to know.

I had until five o'clock the following day to have my column turned in, and I accepted all the bigotry that came from the good white folks of Atlanta and questioned why the blacks still allowed certain shit to carry on.

I was walking around the office for two days after my column debuted with five hundred dollars' worth of gauze around my ass from the chewing I received from the brass upstairs. I couldn't just let my report end with "because this is what we prefer," stated the superintendent. I interviewed city council members, stated that I received a *no comment* from the mayor's office, and reported that the governor's office refused to speak to me or return my faxes on the matter.

Nevertheless, I was given my props after I ended up doing an interview and being pictured in the *Ebony* magazine. After my fame was highlighted for the world to read about, my supervisors were very careful about giving me certain assignments because I didn't know how to "apply the politically correct amount of pressure," so they said. They viewed me as an "overkiller"!

Once this Williams cat was finally caught for killing all those children, I was so into the mainstream of what other reporters considered bullshit. While the killings were going on, I had become the shit of the bullshit. I was receiving award after award, and though I didn't have to ask for certain assignments, I woke up looking at myself as an achiever.

It was Sunday afternoon when I got the call from Aunt Vera informing me that Hope was found dead at the house.

I was awakened by a stewardess asking me to put on my seat belt because we were about to land. For a split second, I felt excitement steering on the inside, that excitement I always felt when I was about to see my sister and my man, Darius. But as I struggled to get my belt on, I felt that sinking feeling again. I had slept for the entire flight, a much-needed sleep, obviously, but now, now the pain was creeping in as I realized I would not see Hope, and I would not be seeing Darius. Hope was gone, and I wasn't going to be allowed within ten feet of Darius until court proceedings were underway.

The first place I stopped was at the Waco Police Department. I knew whoever was in charge of Hope's investigation wasn't going to give me too much information. The case was ongoing, but I was going to get something.

My entry to the regulars was noticed right off. "Can I help you, sir?" asked the desk sergeant.

"My name is Trey Allen, and my sister's name is Hope Allen."

He pushed his glasses back up on his nose. "Give me a few minutes, and I'll have somebody out here to speak with you. Please, have a seat if you don't mind," he said.

"I've been on a flight from Atlanta and a ninety-minute drive from Dallas. No disrespect, but the last thing that I want to do is sit down." I continued to stand, and he shook his head and told me he understood and would quickly get someone out to see me.

I had been in and out of enough police stations to know that a few minutes meant at least ten. About five minutes passed, and a plainclothes officer came through the front door with his hand extended for a greeting. "Mr. Trey Allen, I'm Detective Mark Dunbar, and I'm assigned to your sister's case," he said. He put his hand out and gave me a firm handshake.

"Please, why don't we find an empty office so that we won't be disturbed? Can I get you something to drink?" he asked as we proceeded into the precinct. "Please take a seat, Mr. Allen."

"Trey will be enough, and can we get past your questioning so that I can get to mine, out of respect, if you don't mind?"

"That will be fine with me, Trey. You have an address in Atlanta?" I gave him my address and told Detective Dunbar that the whole newspaper company would verify my being in town. "How did you hear about your sister, and can you give me a time?"

"My aunt Vera called me right after one o'clock this afternoon."

"You wouldn't happen to have your ticket stubs on you?" I was pulling what he wanted out of my pocket before he finished the sentence.

"Were you and Hope pretty tight as siblings?"

"Very much so," I replied.

"What about enemies? She have any?"

"Say, Mark, if you don't mind the first name basis?"

"No, Mark is cool."

"You probably already know that my sister could kick the average man's ass, and I've yet to know a woman that could hold up to her fury because it's all over the house. So if you're questioning her ability to defend herself, cancel that!"

"You still haven't answered the question, Trey."

"No enemies that I can think of."

"What about a reason to want her dead?" he asked.

"Hold on. So you don't buy the overdose shit either, do you?" I asked.

"We'll get to that as soon as I'm finished, Trey."

"She was worth about a hundred grand in finances, and if I know my sister, her son was getting every cent."

"What about her past lady friends and Donald Simms?"

"Kat would be the only one in her past life and Donald's last-known girlfriend. Maybe she could answer that question. Early on in their relationship, I saw Hope's arm bandaged up from fighting with one or two of Donald's girls, but I wouldn't say that they would be or qualify as her enemies though."

"Well, you can never be too sure, Trey. Are you planning on being in town for a few?"

"I'm not leaving this city until I find out what happened to my sister, until I find who did it, and until I get my hands on her son."

"So why would you conclude that someone might have done this to Hope?"

I looked at the detective's statute and arm length. "No harm intended, but if YOU wanted to force-feed Hope some heroin intravenously, this investigation wouldn't be about my sister! So why don't you buy the suicide story?" I asked him.

"For starters, no evidence of her cooking her fix up. It was a sloppy attempt to insert the dope. An addict would shoot, draw back the blood and the heroin into the syringe before they delivered. Her fix was clean. No drawback, and it didn't hit the vein at all."

I sat there listening to this man talk about my sister as if she were just some unknown person, and I was getting information for a story.

He didn't stop and continued, "Plus, we believe that there was some trauma to her head that wasn't due to a fall. Whoever was there with her, she knew because there was no sign of a forced entry. But we won't know more than that until the reports come home from the state medical examiner's office, and that could take a few weeks at best."

"Do you have any leads or a suspect at all?"

"Trey, we're doing the best we can. You're a reporter, you know the rules, and from all the awards I saw over the fireplace at your sister's, you're a damn good one at that. So I'll tell you this in hopes that you'll let us do our jobs. Please don't get in the way or cross paths with me or this department."

"How long have you been a detective, Mark?"

He replied that he was going on seven. "That's a good number. If you haven't arrested the person or persons responsible for Hope's death in seven weeks, consider your grounds trespassed." After informing him of my intent, I got up and walked out of the office.

I felt so helpless, and the fact that I couldn't get my hands on Darius didn't make things any better for me. I had to wait until Monday morning to make my intentions known about Darius, and all I could hear within my thinking was Hope saying, "Trey, please get my baby."

It was late, and I couldn't do anything until morning, and as tired as I was, listening to Aunt Vera all night would be too much for me to deal with right now.

She knew I was making my way into Texas, and for me to keep her worried would be cruel on my part, so I had to call her. Since the La Quinta Hotel was the best thing going and closer to the courthouse, I made my way there. After taking a long hot shower, I dialed Aunt Vera's number and vowed not to let her rob me from the drowsiness that hung on to me like a bad habit.

The phone rang twice, and as the receiver got closer to her face, she called out my name twice. "Trey. Trey, is that you?"

"Yeah, Aunt Vera. It's me!"

"Baby, I've been worried sick about you. Where are you?"

"I'm in town, Aunty. I stopped at the police station to try to find out something about Hope."

"Child, people have made my house into Grand Central Station."

"So do you plan to handle the funeral arrangements?" I asked. I had already gathered that notion when she mentioned everybody coming and going from her home. "I went ahead and made plans to meet with the funeral home in the morning. Baby, I got your room ready for you," she stated.

"Aunt Vera, I'm not staying one night over there. Your phone is constantly ringing, people are coming in and out, and I don't want to deal with all that. So don't get mad either."

She said she understood. "Hope has a safe deposit box with her insurance papers in it, and I won't be able to get them to you until morning, so don't worry about anything," I said.

"Trey, we have to go get the baby. Oh, he was so shook-up and kept reaching out for me to get him, and they wouldn't let me have him," she explained and broke down crying at the same time.

That drew the line for me. "Aunty, calm down and try to get you some rest. I'll be trying to get my hands on him as soon as the courthouse is open."

"So where are you staying tonight, baby?"

"I got a room at the La Quinta, and please keep that between us."

"Child, you and I both know that Jean is going to pitch a fit if you don't call her. So if you don't call her by noon, I'm tellin' her where you are because you know she plays mama to all of us. Hell, she was trippin' because I beat her to the punch on Hope's funeral arrangements."

"I'll be by before noon, and if I'm not there by then, I'm still dealing with Darius."

"Well, get you some rest, and I'll see you tomorrow," she said as she hung up. All I could think about as I slipped into unconsciousness was whoever did this to Hope knew Darius was in the house. The murderer came there for a reason.

The caretakers of the courthouse had the doors open at seven thirty and though I didn't have a clue as to what judge I would have to appear before, by eight ten that wasn't going to be an issue. I was on the pay phone, calling and trying to get a hold of an attorney who would represent me on a short notice. Before eight came to its hour, the pay phone that I was using rang. "This is Trey Allen. Who am I speaking with?"

"Mr. Allen, this is Tim Coleman from Coleman, Johnson, and Reeds. I'll meet you at the county clerk's office in ten minutes, my condolences to you and your family. I don't know if the details stand factual, but you calling my office at this time of the morning and traveling that far for your nephew means you want him, and I'll be willing to see that you get him. Ten minutes and I'll be in an olive green double-breasted suit," he said as he ended the call.

Five minutes later, I spotted Detective Dunbar walking out of the elevator. As soon as he spotted me, he walked my way. "You able to grab some sleep?" he asked as we shook hands.

"I wouldn't call it that, but I'm better off than I was. What brings you down so early?" I asked him.

"I got my money on you getting your nephew, but it's my business to know who else is putting in a bid."

"Who else are you expecting?" I was curious.

"Well, since you arrived, I'm taking both your aunts out of the hat, and if Donald Simms doesn't show up, I'm handing my shield in."

"You see him as a possible suspect?" I asked.

"I'm looking for a motive, Trey! If he might have been part of the reason, then he'll know who and why."

"So you haven't questioned him yet?"

"I plan to do that this morning. In fact, I'm about to do that right this minute," he stated. When the elevator doors opened, we both looked and saw Donald exiting.

"Mr. Allen," came from a voice behind me. I turned to see Mr. Coleman and another staff member following closely behind him.

"That would be me," I stated.

"I'm sorry for the delay, but I had to wait on some information on you to be faxed to me."

"Information on me?" I asked with a high level of suspense.

"I always check up on all my clients, Mr. Allen. No exceptions! You're squeaky clean and a hell of a reputation as a reporter too."

"I can't seem to shake such slanderous conversation these days."

"This young lady is going to be a friend of the judge and your key to getting Darius back without a dilemma. So, Mr. Allen, meet Ms. Sandra Wilson." We shook hands, and from the look on my face, she knew that I wanted Darius today!

"Mr. Allen, relax! If you walk into the judge's chamber wearing that face, the only thing you'll receive is a week of consideration. So relax!"

"The gentleman in the navy blue suit talking to the detective is Donald Simms, also known as Spoon, the ex-pimp turned preacher. He and my sister were dating before God's transformation came down in both their lives. That would be attorney-client privilege?" I waited for him to confirm, and he nodded yes. So I continued, "Darius is his son, but he doesn't know it, and Hope had no plans on telling him."

"Thanks for the heads-up, but if Mr. Simms is being represented by that well-dressed lady there, she might just bring the possibility up. That's Lora Green. Now, if she does, Darius might end up in CPS care for a minute because she is a fighter. If Spoon was a serial killer with good morals and principles, Lora would get a consideration," said Mr. Coleman. "She's just that good."

"Excuse my demeanor, but fuck that! Today, he's a suspect or being considered as one," I cried out.

"In that case, Mr. Allen, consider him fucked!" said Mr. Coleman. "Sandra, find out who holds the keys to this man's nephew, and let's get this dance on."

"Yes, sir," she said as she walked into the clerk's office.

"The detective, does he have a name?" asked Mr. Coleman. I told him it was Mark Dunbar, and Coleman wanted to also know if he was overseeing Hope's case.

"Yeah and stated that he was putting his money on me getting Darius, and he's staying to see the outcome."

"That's just what we need. In fact, he just got into the party for free."

Sandra came rushing out of the clerk's office as if there were a fire in the building. "Judge Evans is giving us thirty minutes of her time without an appointment since Mr. Allen has traveled the distance. She doesn't want him to feel like her hospitality is low rate, and she started her timer."

When we walked up to Mark, Donald, and his no-nonsense of an attorney, Mr. Coleman ended their conversation.

"Mr. Simms, Detective, Lora, I hate to break up your conversation, but Evans has agreed to speak with my client concerning the custody of his nephew. So if you would like to join us, and please, Detective, it would be so kind if you would join us."

"Wouldn't mind if I do, sir, and you would be?" asked Mark.

"Attorney Tim Coleman."

"I want to advise you that this may be a waste of your client's time because my client is here to gain custody of his son," said Lora.

"Not good enough, Lora, and if you or your client don't want to risk Darius being put on hold for weeks, stay in the hallway because my client's sister is dead, he's traveled too far for possibilities of being your client's son, and I haven't had coffee this morning," said Coleman.

"Mr. Allen, I hate that you've come this far to face such a thing and having to deal with the death of your sister as well, but please know that I'm only doing as my client requests," said Lora.

"Twenty minutes, boss," Sandra told Mr. Coleman as she tapped on her watch.

"Let's go get your nephew, Mr. Allen."

The bailiff informed the judge of the added parties, and she came out of her chambers to meet us in her courtroom.

"Good morning, ladies and gentlemen. I will tell you this. As soon as my timer goes off, I will hear no more. Before we proceed, which one of you is Trey Allen?"

"I am, Your Honor," I said as I held up my hand.

"My condolences, sir. Okay, fourteen minutes, people. Mr. Coleman, you're first."

"Your Honor, you are aware that my client has traveled a considerable distance to care for Darius and I have my client's complete background," handing the bailiff Trey's information, "and this will no doubt show the court that Darius deserves to be in the care of Mr. Allen."

"Very impressive, Mr. Allen, but I have no intentions on allowing Mr. Allen to drag this child back to Atlanta this soon," said the judge.

"Your Honor, if I may." I had to interrupt and proceeded after the judge gave me permission. "Your Honor, I'm not leaving this city or state until this investigation concerning my sister's death is concluded, and I don't mean to sound cocky, ma'am, but Darius is now my life. Wherever he is, is where I'll be."

"Ms. Green, you're up," said the judge.

"Your Honor, Mr. Allen has only established himself in Darius's life as an uncle only on his birthday and at Christmas. On the other hand, my client was the last-known boyfriend of the deceased and says that Darius is his biological son. He has spent more time around Darius."

"Mr. Coleman, nine minutes," said the judge.

"Your Honor, time that has been spent around Darius does not constitute the love Mr. Allen has for Darius, and I ask that we not make this a tit-for-tat issue here. Mr. Simms has no knowledge of Darius actually being his son. If we are going to place judgments on our client's merits, then I would prefer that Attorney Green be straight up with the court and inform the court of her client's established merits, please."

"I'm waiting, Ms. Green," stated the judge.

"Your Honor, my client is a reformed solicitor for prostitutes—"

Judge Evans cocked her head and looked at Spoon, then back to his attorney. "You mean a pimp, and a reformed one you said?" asked the judge.

"Yes, Your Honor! He has given his life to the service of God and is now a minister, Your Honor."

"Mr. Coleman," said the judge.

"She forgot to mention that Reverend Simms is also considered a suspect, or in a light note, Your Honor, a person of interest in this investigation."

"Ms. Green," said the judge.

"Your Honor, my client has just been questioned this morning and has yet to be labeled as an interest in any form by the Waco Police Department."

"Detective Dunbar, you have something you want to tell me, sir?" asked the judge.

"Ma'am—"

"You will address me accordingly, Detective."

"Your Honor, Mr. Simms is a matter of interest but not a suspect. As the investigating officer, I strongly believe that someone closely associated in both Hope Allen's life and Mr. Simms's life is involved, but it's only been forty-eight hours, Your Honor."

The timer rang. "Time's up people. Before I make my conclusion in the matter of Darius Allen, I want to know one thing. I recorded the news coverage of an officer handing that crying child over to an emergency medical staff member. This child, now known to me as Darius Allen, was covered in blood from the top of his poor little head to his tiny feet."

Judge Evans paused as if she were holding back her emotions. "With all the people around that bloody child, he reached out numerous times for an elderly lady in the crowd. Do any of you have a clue to who this lady is?"

"If I stand correct, Your Honor, that would be Trey Allen's aunt, and her name is Vera Jenkins," said Detective Dunbar.

"Bailiff, I want this Vera Jenkins standing before me within the next hour," Judge Evans ordered.

"I'm on it, Judge. Would either of you happen to have an address?" the bailiff asked.

"Yes, 6505 Tennyson Drive and her phone number was 555-3107."

The judge was not finished. "If Ms. Vera Jenkins agrees to care for Darius, and from what I saw on TV, she wanted Darius just as badly as Darius wanted her, I will issue judgment and grant full custody to Ms. Jenkins until the investigation is over, and only then will I grant who gets him after that. Have a seat, people, and nobody move until Ms. Jenkins arrives."

I had to take a hard look at Donald, but it wasn't on harming Hope; it was his backbone now that Hope was gone. On top of that, Kat was now on my shit list because she was the only person that could have dripped the facts about Darius to him.

"Are you going to be comfortable with your aunt having custody of Darius, Mr. Allen?" asked Mr. Coleman.

"She's like a mother to me, and I'll be staying with her until I figure out some things."

"Mr. Allen, I'd like to bring something to your attention. I've been a lawyer for more than thirty years, and the only time I have a problem sorting out my gut feeling is when my ulcers start acting up on me. Right now, my ulcers are fine, and I'm as sure as the sun setting this afternoon that Mr. Simms wants that child for personal reasons, and it's not honorable."

"Mr. Coleman, Hope always told me that my success was only built on my being nosy. I've yet to get a gut feeling about Donald, but when I do, I assure you, I won't ignore it, and I'll keep your concerns close."

Lora Green was approaching our privacy, and with the look Donald had on his face, I knew it was going to concern him. "Sorry to intrude, but I'd like to know if you would concede to my client having visiting rights?"

Coleman and I looked at each other for a split second. "Excuse me," I said as I brushed past Ms. Green to check Donald's weak ass.

"Mr. Allen, that's not how we conduct things in court," Lora stated as she attempted to stop me. I really wasn't trying to flex on the brother with an attitude, but someone killed Hope, and my nephew was in the hands of some stranger, and this bitch wanted to play footsies at the wrong time.

I looked back at Lora with a stony look on my face. "You've got two seconds to remove your finger off my sleeve." She did so without another thought. "Off the record, Counselor, court for a black man under my conditions is where his feet stop. So if you'll excuse me, I need to take a few more steps," I said as I headed toward Donald.

"Let's get one thing straight. I've never given a damn about you, and I still don't. I've tolerated your ass because my sister cared about you. You've brought your ass in here today, trying to push up on the only thing I have left outside of my aunts as if you didn't know what has just happened to Hope two days ago. You are either a coldhearted bastard or you just don't give a damn, but either way, don't play games with me right now as if I've turned into a soft-ass nigga. You'll have plenty of time to see Darius in church if you want to know or see how he's doing. Outside of that, don't fuck with me behind my family, and in fact, you need to get your ass out of this courtroom with this good reverend bullshit before I lose my cool."

We both stared eye to eye at each other for about ten seconds.

"Gentlemen, this is not either the time or place for this," said Mr. Coleman.

"Jesus loves you, brother, and so do I, Trey," Donald said as he started to leave the courtroom.

"You fuck yourself," I replied.

Lora Green escorted Donald out of the courtroom, telling him that he did not have to accept such a treatment, and she could bring it to the judge's attention, but Donald was no fool! I knew Lora wasn't leaving the building because the judge gave us strict orders to sit.

I took a seat alone, away from where Sandra and Mr. Coleman were, to calm down. "What was he after?" I asked myself, and the only thing that I could remotely come up with was Hope's money.

A few minutes later, Aunt Vera came through the door, escorted by two deputies. She came over to me with her eyes welled up with tears. "Hey, baby! Boy, when you say you gone do something, you mean it!" she said.

"It wasn't me, Aunty. You did it by being on the news. The judge will only give Darius to you."

"Well, she needs to hurry up then because I know that child is a nervous wreck right now."

"Well, you won't have to wait to much longer because she's coming through the door right now," I stated before walking Aunt Vera up to the front of the courtroom.

"Would you happen to be Ms. Vera Jenkins?" asked the judge.

Aunt Vera said she was.

"Darius must love you very much and know you when he sees you," said Judge Evans.

Aunt Vera started crying.

"Ms. Jenkins, why are you crying, ma'am?" asked the judge.

"Darius ain't happy where he is, and the poor child needs his family right now."

"So you will be more than willing to care for Darius until all matters are settled concerning the death of his mother?" asked the judge even though she knew the answer.

"Young lady, I don't mean no disrespect when it comes to this courtroom stuff, but I'm old enough to be your mother. You look me in the eyes as another woman as I say this too, but you need to give me that baby today if you have a caring heart," said Aunt Vera.

"Well, Ms. Jenkins, I knew you were the right person to look after him when I saw the both of you on the television. While my bailiff was escorting you here, I also had Darius brought to my chambers. You're very correct, Ms. Jenkins. Darius is very agitated and needs his family. I will inform you that I will be checking up on him from time to time."

"Young lady, you're welcomed at my home day or night, child," said Aunt Vera, and the judge started laughing.

"Ms. Jenkins, I'll take you up on your offer one day, but for now, you'll have to sign some paperwork before you leave. Right now, I want you to calm Darius down for me," the judge stated as she motioned the deputy to retrieve the CPS worker who had Darius.

When the door opened that led back to the judge's chambers, you could hear Darius crying. Aunt Vera put her purse down and took off toward his plea. Once Darius spotted Aunt Vera, his little arms stretched out toward her, and he begged to be rescued.

After about three minutes with Aunt Vera, Darius was almost asleep, and the talking in the courtroom was down to a whisper as Darius found refuge in Aunt Vera's arms.

The judge allowed me to sign all the necessary paperwork to take Darius home. It was after ten o'clock before I got Darius and Aunt Vera back home. I had to get back out of the house to go to the bank for

Hope's insurance papers. I gather this was a good time for Aunt Vera to share some responsibilities with Aunt Jean. Aunt Vera having Darius was like being crowned aunt of the century, and she was wearing her crown very well!

After leaving the bank, I headed down to the eastside of Waco. In order for a sister to blend in and not look too out of place, a low-down hoe would be in her natural habitat. Elm Street or the Old Dallas Highway was a common hoe stroll, and I wasn't about to put Kat on hold another minute.

I rode up and down Elm Street before heading toward the Old Dallas Highway. I spotted Kat leaning inside of a car that was parked at a two-bit motel. As soon as she saw my face, something came over her whole demeanor.

She never turned her attention back toward her trick but came straight to me. It was clearly evident that her lifestyle had dropped to an all-time low. She looked as if she was pulled out from the depths of hell. I was parked on the other side of the street, and she had to dart traffic to get to me, but she pranced as if she was still holding on to that 34-21-38.

From the looks of her, her proportions had diminished down to a mere 22-15-24 and was halfway dead. I got out of the car to ensure vice or any passing patrol car that I was not trying to score a favor on their beat. "Hey, baby," she said as she walked toward me, arms up and expecting a hug.

"Kat, you know how I feel about being handled when you ain't right."

"I'm sorry, daddy. I'm just happy when I see your fine ass." She kept wiping her hands on her thin legs and looked down to the ground like she was searching for the words she was trying to say. "Trey, I'm sorry about Hope. I've been sick about that since I heard about it."

"Kat, why did you tell Spoon?"

"Tell him what, daddy?" Kat looked up at me with sunken eyes.

"Don't fuck with me, Kat!" I didn't mean to shout, but I couldn't help it.

"Trey, look at me. I'm bad off, baby. He wanted to know for sure, and two hundred dollars stood between that answer. So I told him, Trey."

"You and I know Hope wasn't into no dope, right?" I asked her.

"I know, daddy."

"So who did it, Kat?" She gave me that diva look and placed her hand on whatever hips she had left.

"How the fuck am I supposed to know, Trey?"

"So you tellin' me you don't know shit, Kat?"

"I don't know shit, Trey. I swear!"

"That wouldn't be the same 'swear' you gave Hope about not telling Spoon about Darius, would it?"

"Fuck you, Trey. You didn't have to go there."

"Kat, I swear, when all of this is over with, and I find out that you knew something about this, I hope you burn in hell," I said as I got back into my car.

"I'm already in hell, Trey," she shouted as I drove off.

Kat just let me know that it was about feeding her addiction, so anything goes right now. Being the dope fiend that she was, she wouldn't have shot Hope up like that without doing it right. So she didn't push the dope in Hope.

As bad as I wanted to find some peace back at the La Quinta, I knew that was all I was going to get for a long time. When I finally got back over to Aunt Vera's house, she and Aunt Jean were in the kitchen, talking. They never knew I was in the house. I knew Darius would be in her bed, so I went straight there.

I tried to sit down on the bed beside him as easy as I could without waking him up, but he popped his eyes open and just stared at me with a little smile on his face.

"Hi there, little man. You act like you don't know your uncle anymore. That's okay because I know you've been through hell these past few days. I want you to know that I'm not going anywhere, and we both gonna get through this together. Your mama loved you very much, Darius, and don't you ever forget that. Whoever did that to your mother,

Uncle Trey gonna make sure they don't get away. Okay?" Tears ran down my face as I tried to assure him that it would be okay.

I guess he felt my pain because he rose up and hugged my neck. For a split second, I felt Hope's arms around me too.

"Let me stop being the baby. Hell, you've cried enough for all of us these past few days," I told him as I carried him to the bathroom. "You know how to use one of these?" I asked him as I unzipped his pants and pulled his little pride out to pee.

He wasn't tall enough, so I held his small frame up over the toilet, and he took care of his business like a pro. "Now we have to wash our hands, but I know that means playing in the water for you."

I carried him to the dining room table, and my aunts were surprised to know that I was even in the house. I handed Darius to my aunt Jean after I gave her a kiss. "The both of you were carrying on so deep in your conversation. I just went to check on my boy."

"Here are Hope's insurance papers and a thousand dollars to buy her something nice to put on." I placed everything in the center of the table to avoid getting caught in the middle of an aunty war. Neither one of them made a move toward the money or her policy, but I knew they both wanted to pounce on the change to claim responsibility.

"I need the both of you to listen to me real close. I don't want Donald to be alone with Darius. He can do or say whatever he wants to, as long as Darius is with one of you, and I don't want the whole church to know how I feel about this either."

"Vera May, Trey just implied that we talked too much!" whimpered my aunt Jean.

"Girl, stop acting like we don't," Aunt Vera said.

"Has he done something wrong, Trey?" Aunt Vera asked.

I couldn't tell them what I knew because I knew they couldn't hold water. "Naw, Aunty, but he made me mad coming up in the courtroom, trying to get custody of Darius as if either one of us wasn't coming to get him," I replied.

"Well, you do what you can to help these people find out who did this to that child, and let us worry about Darius."

Looking Back

It had been seven days since Hope was stripped away from Darius. I found myself staring down at Darius as he slept. It was very difficult for me to place myself in his shoes because I couldn't fathom not having Mama when I was his age. Since he was only two years old, no one would ever know what he really felt or the level of burdens that he was about to experience.

Nevertheless, I had made up my mind that it was time for me to move back home. Taking Darius away from all his roots would be making a statement that nothing in his past meant anything.

Hope's autopsy was due in this morning, and I already knew that Mark Dunbar had firsthand knowledge on Hope's cause of death because the crime scene investigators were back at the house for at least twelve hours.

Whatever they were looking for had something to do with the cause of Hope's death, or they were looking for direct ties to a suspect. It was too early for Dunbar to call me at home since it was only six thirty in the morning. I waited by the phone.

On top of all that, the funeral home brought Hope's body in last night at about ten, and the only reason why I didn't rush to see her was because I knew the uncut sight of a post-autopsy would be a cruel sight for me. The owner of the funeral home told me that she would be presentable by noon today, so I was cool with that.

"Boy, you watch over that baby like a mother does." Aunt Vera was standing in the door, watching us both. "Outside of you and Jean, he's all I have left. I've always wondered why the members in this family died so early in life. I look back on it all and ask God why, but all I've received was another funeral to go to."

"You and Aunt Jean are the oldest relatives to live as long as you have. Hell, Darius and I need to start sippin' on some of that longevity ya'll been stashing and holding back on." Aunt Vera found that funny.

"Baby, it's called prayer," she said.

"Haven't done too much of that in the past, but the way this past week has gone, I feel the need to put in some work," I stated as I walked toward the kitchen for a shot of coffee.

It was funny seeing Darius walk side-by-side with Aunt Vera, and no matter how much love he had for his uncle Trey, if Aunt Vera moved, he moved! He came up to me, wanting to get picked up because he wanted a good look at what was on the table. I hadn't just totally weaned myself off fresh doughnuts, and now that I was back at home, there was nothing I'd rather have than some Jack 'N' Jill Donuts.

Darius knew that if I was at the table early in the morning, glazed treats were close by. Aunt Vera wasn't trying to hear that though. It was a real breakfast for him, and the doughnut came after he ate his lunch.

The phone was ringing, and Aunt Vera and I just stared at each other past the fourth ring. We both knew who it was and what was being delivered. I answered it on the sixth ring.

I answered the phone, saying, "Jenkins's residence."

"Trey, Mark Dunbar. I didn't wake you, did I?"

"To be honest, Mark, I had to breathe before answering the phone because I knew it was you. Give it to me straight, Mark."

"It wasn't from an overdose. Whoever did it was in a rush because they missed the vein. She died from a blow to the head by some sort of blunt object. Penetrated the skull just enough to cause brain swelling."

He let this news soak in a second, then continued, "Whoever did it also broke the coffee table in the living room to make it look like she overdosed and struck her head on the table, thus causing the table to break. I sent my lab boys back in one more time and came up with the same findings."

"So what is that supposed to mean, Mark?"

"We either charge Darius or your two aunts for the murder of your sister, or we keep looking!"

"You've got to be bullshitin' me." I had to stop myself from hitting the wall. I was so frustrated, but I didn't want to upset Aunt Vera and especially not Darius.

"Trey, it's still early in the investigation, buddy, and anything can pop up to give us what we need, so don't give up on us. I assure you that I'm not stopping until we come up with the answer to who did this to your sister."

I paused for a second just to catch my breath. I couldn't believe I was hearing what was coming from his mouth. I had to remind myself of who I was and tell myself that this particular case was far bigger to me than the Atlanta murders. "I have to go get a job, Mark. I want you to know that I'm officially back on my block. We can either work together or you can have my black ass locked up for interfering in this investigation."

"I'm surprised you stood still this long, Trey, but you foul my tracks up, and you'll be in a six-by-nine cell until I solve this case."

"Save all the dramatics, Detective. By Monday afternoon, I'll be a reporter for the *Herald*, and my first scoop will be Hope Allen. Again, we either do this shit together or I'm on my own, your call."

"I'll meet with you after the funeral," Mark said and hung up the phone. He knew he had given me enough to spark my drive, and outside of the antics, he was asking for some help anyway. We both knew that the answer to Hope's murder wasn't inside of my parents' home but in the streets. I looked at Darius and knew he had the answers.

"Boy, are you going to stare at Darius all day, or are you going to tell me what the man said?" asked Aunt Vera.

"Somebody hit Hope in the head with something and killed her."

"I knew that girl wasn't on that stuff and whoever wrote that story in the paper about her needs to be fired," Aunt Vera said as she started humming and working to get Darius's breakfast ready.

"Turn around here, little man," I said to Darius. "You know who was in the house with mommy, don't you?"

"Mommy, Mommy," he said as he squeezed my nose.

"Yeah, you know who it was but don't have a clue to what's going on. Well, Uncle Trey is going to help you out, nephew," I told him as I kissed his cheek and sat him in his own personal chair.

"I have to run, Aunt Vera. I'll be checkin' in on Darius after twelve, and I'll tell the funeral home about the funeral being Monday."

"Do what you have to do, baby. You serious 'bout that job at the paper?"

"That's the only legal way I can get into the realm of finding out who did this to Hope."

As I left Aunt Vera's, I had full intentions to head straight to the *Herald*, but I had to see how much protection Waco's finest had on my mother's place. As soon as I drove past the house, I saw the tape across the door, indicating the presence of an ongoing investigation. I knew the only way that I was going to get into the house was through Dunbar, or I would have to cross the police line without authority.

That would surely land my ass in jail, and I wasn't about to risk that because, one thing Dunbar said that made sense, things were fresh, and anything could pop up at any moment. First things first, a job!

As soon as I entered the lobby, I was greeted at the center of the corridor by a security guard asking if he could help me.

"I'm here to see the editor or editor in charge. My name is Mr. Trey Allen from the Atlanta papers," I replied with a sense of pride.

"Is he expecting you, Mr. Allen?"

"Indeed he is, sir," I said, knowing I was lying, but I knew once my name was passed on I was going to be given access.

"Mr. Peterson, I have a Mr. Trey Allen here in the lobby." Whatever he was asked, it was "yes, sir" and "yes, sir" before I was handed a visitor's tag. "I gather you already know how to find your way up, right?" asked the security guard. I took the tag and shook his hand and thanked the good man.

As I got into the elevator, I had one thing on my mind, a compromise for my skills, and that meant polishing up Hope's image that some asshole smeared with shit and sticking with the whole investigation until it was said and done. As the elevator doors rolled open, Mr. Peterson was right outside of them with his arms folded across his chest and glasses pulled down over his nose.

"How you doing, Pete?" I asked him when I stepped off the elevator. "I should be asking you that question, Trey," he said as we hugged each other.

"Sorry for your loss, brother," he offered. We walked to his office, and once we made it inside, he drew the blinds to give us some much-needed privacy. Whether or not his working staff knew who I was, all eyes were on us when we walked into his office.

"I don't want you to think that I'm asking you a silly question, but do you already have the results on your sister's autopsy report?" Peterson asked.

"Got it about an hour ago," I replied. I found Peterson asking me that question kind of odd, and I couldn't let this slide. "You know something I don't, Pete?"

"Son, I was hoping you'd give me some insight as to why Waco PD would ask me to hold off until tomorrow before I print the results."

"No shit!" I said with some curiosity dripping off by brow. "You thinking what I'm thinking?" asked Peterson.

"Pete, if you were going to arrest someone, it would be on the wire. Plus, I spoke with the lead dick this morning, and he stated that he sent his CSI squad in for a second run and found nothing. So why the stall tactics is a good question!" I said.

Dunbar putting me on hold until Monday let me know he wasn't ready to lay all his cards on the table. Then again, with the public knowing that Hope was hit in the head, wherever the murder weapon was or whoever had it was about to make sure it didn't surface again.

Peterson wanted to know if I knew who Donald Simms was, and I wanted to know why he wanted to know. "PD is searching his home right now, heard the address over the scanner. I just okayed the section on your sister, and after the funeral home told us her funeral service was going to be at 3107 Brewster Street, and the address over the scanner was 3109 Brewster Street, I told myself this had to be church property. As soon as my man reached the scene, Mr. Simms was being held on the curb by two dicks, and the house was being searched. I did the honors of running his name through and was pretty impressed. Petty theft, a few arrests for assaults that never made it to court, and a pimp but a minister on top of all that!"

"He and my sister used to date before the pulpit came into play, and for the record, she wasn't in the streets, Pete."

"So what brings you here, Trey?"

"I need a job, Pete. I'm not concerned with the pay issue, but I want full exclusives on my sister, and I do nothing else until this is over with."

"You're hired," he said as he quickly sat up in this chair. "You looking for a cover just to meddle in the police department's business or do you want a job?" Peter asked to get a confirmation on whether I was going to be a part of his crew on a temporary basis or not.

"Pete, I'm home for a while, my friend. I can't see myself dragging my nephew around, and you know what my work is like. I have family here, and he needs all of us. Do we have a deal or not?" He stood up and shook my hand. "Deal!" he replied.

I made arrangements to come in sometime after the funeral to take care of all my paperwork. No matter how I was feeling after Hope's funeral, my having to bury Hope was my fuel to help catch this person.

After leaving the *Herald*, heading over to the eastside of Waco to view Hope's body meant spotting Kat. I thought more than a few times about putting her ass into my car, taking her somewhere, and handcuffing her down until she told me something. Though I haven't seen a sick heroin addict without his fix, from what I've heard, the pangs are so bad that they rather choose death than go through the withdrawal.

I just couldn't see myself torturing Kat like that, and like she said, she was already in hell! Pulling up at the funeral home was a moving experience for me because Hope quickly let me know that she was in my presence. I felt some of the coldest chills I'd ever felt in my life. *I know you're here, Hope, and Darius is okay. I know if you could talk to me or give me some kind of indication who did this to you, you would. I won't give up though!* I got out of my car to walk inside to see her.

I don't know if morticians practice the art of smiling their horror-tale smile, but the greeting that I was receiving from the owner of the establishment was wicked. "You must be Mr. Allen?" The first thing that crossed my mind was *Damn, the SOB is psychic too!* "How'd you know?" I asked as I shook his chilled hand.

"Facial structure, it's just like your sister's."

"You know that shit sounded kind of creepy, huh?" He just laughed and walked me to where Hope lay.

"I tell you, if it's not the stare, cold hand, the slow walk, the slow wave, the smile, or tone of speech, it's always something creepy about me, and I'm the friendliest guy in town," he confessed as we approached Hope's body. "Okay, add that to your list too!" I said, and we both laughed. For me, it was a nervous laugh.

I couldn't believe that I was staring down at my sister, so gentle and serene, lying there lifeless. "The wound to her head, where is it?" I asked the owner.

"It's on the left temple area, but my embalmer did an excellent job of stitching the wound close and covering it up. I realize that no one would be able to see it unless they leaned over into the casket, but we felt it was necessary."

The person was right-handed. "You have any other visitors in here viewing her?" I asked.

"Well, to be honest, Mr. Allen, yes, and the woman wasn't a pretty sight either," he replied. *Kat!* "How long ago?" I asked.

"About an hour or so. Girl ran out saying 'I'm sorry, I'm sorry' repeatedly and crying her heart out."

I reached down into the casket and touched Hope's cold and stiff face. *I love you, girl. I have to go, and you know I won't stop until I catch whoever did this. Rest, Hope!*

"I'll be transporting her body over to Mt. Zion Hill in about an hour as requested by your aunt."

"Whatever she wants," I told him. I shook the brother's hand before leaving and didn't notice the chill.

As I exited the funeral home, I had one thing on my mind. Kat! I rode up and down both strolls for two hours before I spotted her ass getting out of a trick's car. I was up on her before she even realized it. That was a telltale sign that she had just fixed.

"I'm glad to know that you went to see Hope. I'm really waiting to see if loyalty is going to override your need to feed. While you're out here doing what you do, be a goddamn woman for once in your life, and let some type of motherhood kick in. As a man, I wouldn't know the feeling, but do you, Kat? Despite the dope and all the tricks, you can feel instinctively, and you can't avoid that. Think about Darius, Kat, long and hard," I said, before driving off.

As I proceeded up Elm Street, I saw her staring at me through my rearview mirror, and she never moved out of the spot I left her in. As far off as she was, I could feel her presence still. I made my way up to the police station to see Dunbar before I made it any farther into North Waco.

Walking through the door of the station, the same desk sergeant eyeballed me before I could make it past the public sitting area. He was on the phone with Dunbar before I could get to the desk. As I approached the desk, he handed me a visitor's tag. "Through the double doors, take the elevator up to the second floor," he stated with a permanent frowned face.

As I was buzzed through the double doors, I told myself that if Dunbar didn't mention crashing in on Spoon's crib, I was going to start leaving his ass in the dark on shit too. The elevator doors came open, and he waved me over to this desk. "So what brings you to my neck of the woods?" he asked. We did the usual handshake. I was hoping that he would start giving me a lot more credit than what he was willing too.

"I'm officially on the *Herald*'s payroll, and like a good journalist, we know and find out certain shit people in your line of work do. So can we get past the rhetoric format for a change?"

"We didn't find anything, if that's what you want to know," he stated frustratingly.

"So what made you want to take a closer look at him, anyway?" I asked.

"It was just a hunch, really. He wanted the kid too bad. If the kid was the only person who could identify the killer, I would try to get him too! Unfortunately, not even my lab crew could come up with anything."

"I've had two encounters with one of Donald's ex-girls, and I'd stake my reputation on her knowing something," I said.

"You want me to bring her in for a chat?" Dunbar asked as he placed his hand on his phone.

"Not just yet. I figure the closer to Hope's funeral she gets, the more emotional she'll get. I thought she was straddling the fence because she told Donald that Darius was his, but the funeral home director witnessed her leaving the funeral home crying and saying 'I'm sorry' a couple of times." I had to plant a seed.

"Whether it's going to manifest into something or not, I'm betting that she'll come around by Monday or Tuesday. Deep down inside, she really cared about Hope, but her addiction is taking center stage right now."

"I'll give her until Tuesday, and after lunch, I'm bringing her ass in!" Dunbar assured me.

"Look, I need access into my mother's house."

"That's not happening, brother, so don't go there. It's still a crime scene, and though we've been over it twice, I'm not ready to release it yet, at least not until after a couple more weeks."

"Well, I thought I would try," I stated, then I got up to leave.

"Just so you'll know, I'm having my boys outside of the church the day of the funeral." I looked at him with a puzzled face. "I just want to sift through your guest, run some plates, but I won't be interested in any unpaid traffic warrants, so relax." I left Dunbar to go get some much-needed sleep.

I was a thought away from finding refuge back at the La Quinta, but I couldn't be away from Darius. With Hope being back in the city and two days away from her funeral, it was a matter of time before Aunt Vera's house turned into a drive-through.

Darius, Aunt Vera, and Aunt Jean were out on the front porch when I drove up. As soon as I got out of the car and Darius recognized me, he started to bounce up and down with excitement. "Yeah, boy, it's Uncle Trey in the house," I sang. I picked him up and asked my aunts if he'd had a snack for today and kissed them both on their cheeks.

"Child, if you leave it up to one of us to give him some junk food, he'll never get it," Aunt Jean stated.

"Come on, nephew, let Uncle Trey put you down with a serious hookup, boy." Whether his joy for my companionship was general love or knowing he was going to get some sugar from me didn't matter to me because we were kickin' it!

I sat him in his chair, and his eyes followed every move I made as if he was memorizing the stash spots. I hooked his little behind up with four doughnut holes from Jack 'N' Jill Donuts and a scoop of Blue Bell homemade vanilla ice cream. I knew he knew that he was about to get a hookup because he was about to come out of his seat to get it as I turned to put the container of ice cream back in the freezer.

"Whoa there, youngster! You fall out of this chair, and I'll get skinned alive by Aunt Jean and Aunt Vera, boy!" He let me know that I wasn't talking about anything, and the only thing that mattered was what was in that bowl. Once he got his first delivery and got past the chill of the ice cream, it was a wrap! "Keep it coming" is what he implied without having to say a single word, and I allowed him to get his snack on.

When he saw that it was all gone, he looked up at me with a "man is that all" look on his face, and I couldn't help but laugh at his ass because he was putting in some work without a safety hat on. "All gone, Darius," I tried to convince him, so I allowed him to handle the bowl himself. "Gone bye-bye?" he asked, looking at me and then back into the bowl. "Yeah, gone bye-bye, nephew."

After I cleaned him up, I took him back out to my aunts. "I've got to get me some much-needed sleep," I stated, handing Darius over to my aunt Jean.

"So how did she look?" Jean asked.

"She looked real nice and not too much makeup either," I told them.

"Well, she ought to be in the church in about an hour. You have any idea why the police would be in and out of Reverend Simms's house?" Aunt Vera asked with a frowned-up face.

"I can't speak on that, and I would appreciate it if you two would not question or discuss the matter with your church members any further. I'm sure Donald will address the congregation in the morning." Not leaving either of them any room for rebuttal on the matter, I quickly turned and walked away. As nosy as they were, they were going to find out what they wanted to know even if they had to call Donald himself!

It was going on eleven o'clock Sunday morning when I finally decided to get up. The only thing that I can remember was getting up to use the restroom and saying no to Aunt Vera about not wanting to eat breakfast this morning. She made sure that I was awake before they left for church.

I gather everybody was going to turn out for church today because Hope's body was in the conference hall for viewing. The evening service was canceled because Hope's body was being moved into the chapel for public viewing after the regular service. I, on the other hand, had no intentions on seeing her again until the day of the funeral.

It had been a long time since I had a good home-cooked meal. As a result, Aunt Vera and Aunt Jean went out of their way to bless me with a good Sunday dinner. Aunt Jean had decided to open up her home to friends and distant relatives so that I could have some peace and quiet at Aunt Vera's after the funeral.

Darius and I had been playing and goofing off all day, and nightfall had slipped upon me before I even knew it. Aunt Vera was part of the old-school clique and that meant early to bed for both her and Darius and early to rise.

I decided to catch the local news for the first time since I set foot in the city. Nothing big was happening, and though I was enjoying the rest from all the hustle and bustle I was doing in Atlanta, I was bored. Subconsciously, I fought tooth and nail about following Dunbar's orders about not going in Mama's house, but I had to.

There was a fitness center about two blocks away from my parents' house, and it stayed open twenty-four hours a day. I quickly changed clothes and got into some "I don't want to be seen shit" and found my way to the fitness center. I parked so far back into the parking lot that all I had to do was get out of my car and cross the intersection that led to the house.

Just to make sure Dunbar didn't have the house staked out, I jogged one street over before coming down our street. As always, the block was quiet as I approached the house. Though some neighbor's dogs were barking, it wasn't enough to alarm anyone. I wasn't about to enter through the front door so I went around to the back door that led into the garage.

I should have known that something wasn't right when I stuck the key in the door and found the door was already unlocked. I took it as someone from the police department failing to lock it at some point.

Finding the door that led into the house from within the garage also open was too coincidental for me. Being in some of the roughest neighborhoods in Atlanta while working on a story, I learned to carry my gun, and though I never had to use it, it was second nature to carry it.

By the time I drew my pistol to take the safety off, I was struck across the head by a blunt object and knocked to my knees. All I remember after that was someone running out the garage and the sound of iron landing on the concrete. By the time I got my bearings back to slightly normal, whoever it was was long gone.

I had to get the hell out of the house because all the dogs in a two-block radius were raising hell. I stumbled out of the house like a drunk and hoped like hell the moisture that I was feeling around my shoulders, chest, and back was sweat and not blood from the blow I took.

I was concentrating on trying to stay focused so much that I made it back to my car and wasn't aware that I still carried my gun in my hand. I quickly turned on the interior light of the car to see if I was bleeding, and after I saw that I wasn't, I stashed my gun under my car seat and rested awhile.

It was four twenty-three in the morning when I came to and feeling as if a train had dragged me ten miles. The parking lot was nearly empty, and I was wondering why the owners of the cars that were parked next to me didn't check to see if I was all right. On the cool, I was glad they didn't report me to the caretakers of the fitness center.

It was almost five o'clock when I pulled into the driveway. My intention was to rest for a few minutes before going in the house, and two hours later, Aunt Vera was tapping on the window and calling my name. "Trey . . . Trey, baby, open up the door so that I can help you." I stared at her and heard every word she was saying to me but couldn't respond.

I finally unlocked the door after two minutes of pleading instructions from Aunt Vera. "Child, what you done got yourself into, and you bleeding too, boy. Sit still while I call for an ambulance."

"No ambulance, Aunty. Just get me in the house."

"Child, I've lost your father, mother, and your sister, and now you sittin' here bleeding from somewhere and don't even know your own name. Don't you die on me," she said as she helped me out of the car and into the house.

Once she got me in, she scrambled to find some first aid supplies and came back into my room with a large bowl of hot water and a towel. "Get yourself out of that shirt, baby, because you staining up everything." By my jersey being black, it was hard for her to tell where my injury might have been.

"It's my head, Aunty," I said as I placed her hand on the wound. "Boy, you got a knot on your head the size of a plum."

"Do I need stitches?" I asked. I flinched at every touch while she cleaned around the area. "If I can get you to stand still for a second, maybe I can see. It's not that bad, but you have all the signs of a concussion if I ever saw one, and I would go to the hospital if I were you."

"No hospital, Aunt Vera!"

"Me asking you what happened would be a waste of time. You lucky that you have a hard head because whoever did this could have killed you." She fussed at me and poured peroxide on my wound at the same time. "You want the bleeding to stop? Then I have to get down to the cut and that means cutting some hair."

"Do what you have to, but don't make it look bad. I don't want people asking me questions at the funeral."

An hour went by, and I had less than four hours left before the start of Hope's funeral. All I could do was sleep. Aunt Vera woke me up at ten sharp. I thought the hot shower I took before going to sleep would ease the tension on my shoulders, but I was still being dragged by that train.

Evidently, Dunbar's people couldn't have done a good job searching for whatever they were looking for because somebody came back to collect something, and whoever it was had not planned on getting caught.

Whoever it was knew that the investigators didn't find "it." Whatever "it" was, I was standing in the way of freedom, and from what I was feeling, the criminal wasn't trying to give that up!

The funeral home had sent a limousine to pick up Aunt Jean before picking up Aunt Vera, Darius, and me. It was already eleven, and we were just getting in the limousine. Outside of Darius carrying on, the ride to the church was quiet. Like any other function that brothers and sisters attended, there were those who hung outside.

It was easy spotting Waco's finest as we got out of the limousine. By it being after eleven o'clock, I knew Dunbar wasn't keeping that good of an eye on my parents' house. If he had known I was there, he would have been in my face before I left Aunt Vera's, or he would have been watching me go in the church while letting me know that he wanted to see me once the funeral was over with.

Getting past the regular Mt. Zion Hill members who darted out of their seats to show their respect, Donald and I kept constant eye contact with each other until I took my seat. I was concerned about how Darius was going to take this, so I signaled Aunt Jean to send him to me, and the way he came trotting to me was up his alley. He found his spot on my lap and never moved again.

I never figured out what it was about black folks and gospel songs at funerals. Everybody was fine the whole time Reverend Benson was giving Hope's eulogy and through that bullshit Donald spoke about, but as soon as the church's soloist started singing "His Eye Is on the Sparrow," people started unraveling. They were falling out, screaming, and yelling.

"Hope, come back to me," one screamed.

"Hope, get up, Hope," another woman yelled, stumbling and bumping the casket.

By the time it was our turn to view Hope's body, I picked Darius up and was hesitant to show him Hope in the state she was in. Hell, he was already trippin' on everybody else crying. Nevertheless, we stood over Hope for the last time.

"Mama," he said as he looked at me.

"Yeah, little man, that's Mama." Darius started reaching down for her.

"Mama, give me. Give me, Mama," he demanded repeatedly.

"No, Darius. Mama is gone, little man," I said to him.

He looked back up to me with tears in his eyes and he kept saying, "I want it. I want it. Give me, Mama."

That was the last straw! Darius and I went to our awaiting limo with the scene of him holding on to me and me holding on to him as we both cried.

It wasn't until we left the church that Darius calmed down, and when we got to Hope's burial site, Darius and I stayed in the car until everything was over. I wasn't about to subject him to anything else at Hope's funeral.

It wasn't long before we were being dropped back off at Aunt Vera's. A brown Ford Granada was parked in front of the house. As soon as the limo driver opened the door for us, a young scruffy-looking brother emerged from the car. He didn't bother to come any farther than the front of his car. "I have a package for a brother named Trey," he yelled.

I walked up to him with my hand held out to receive the package.

"Oh no, brother. This ain't that type of party. You need to show me some ID and give me some change."

My gorilla instinct wanted to snatch the box right out of his hands, but I was still trying to keep my focus due to my head injury. I went into my pocket and pulled out fifty dollars. "Here's my ID, man. Now give me the damn package." The guy took the money and handed me the package and was off.

I looked at the package and questioned who it might have come from because the label gave no clue. It just had the address and my name on it. It wasn't hard noticing Aunt Vera's extra nosiness getting the best of her, and to deprive her would be cruel. So I handed her the package.

"I don't know who it's from or what's in it," I said. I at least thought she would play her nosiness down just a notch, but that was an understatement in its entirety! She had the box open and the contents out before I could put the key in the door. "Oh look, Trey, some pictures of Hope, Darius, some woman, and Reverend Simms too." I quickly turned to glance down into the photo album and knew who sent it. "Kat," I whispered.

"I need to see those when you're done," I told Aunt Vera as I took the box out of her hand. Kat had left a note for me as well.

Trey,

Despite what you may think about me, I do care about Hope and Darius too! I hate that my life has come to this, but I'm too far in at this point. You'll always be the finest man I've ever seen. I know these pictures will come in handy for you one day soon.

Love, Kat

Sign Language

I guess my brief conversation with Kat was enough to override the monster that had such a horrendous grip on her soul. From the looks of the photo album, she had been around Hope and Darius more than I had. Pictures of her, Hope, and Darius in the hospital as a newborn, his first spoon-feeding, him turning over, his first six months, Darius crawling, and his first birthday party—Kat really loved Hope and Darius. It was also evident that somewhere along the way she made the worst mistake of her life.

The phone rang four times, and I was hesitant to answer the damn thing because it was never for me. I knew once it rang for the fifth time, Aunt Vera was either napping, in the restroom, or too busy dealing with Darius. So I answered it.

"Jenkins' residence."

"Trey, Peterson. How you holding up, buddy?"

"To be honest, I'm dealing with more than what I expected, Pete."

"After you left out the church the way that you did, I got kind of worried about you."

"Pete, tell me this call isn't concerning me and the job."

From the sound of his voice, I got the impression that he was worried that I wasn't going to take the job. He and I both knew that I was not returning to Atlanta and opting out for a job at the *Herald*.

"Aaah come on, Trey! You've got to give me just an ounce of credit," he replied.

"Even that might be too much, Pete. So what gives?"

"Unless your address has changed or the dispatcher at the station blurted out the wrong address over the air, it was your address or at least your mom's old place."

"What time was this, Pete?"

"Right after midnight! With the size of that knot on the back of your head made me want to see if you're doing okay."

"Pete, I was surely considering giving your ass at least an ounce of info, but you just screwed that up. You could have just asked me what happened last night and bypassed the rest of the bullshit," I said just before someone knocked on the door. I rose to take a peep out of the window to see who it was. "Pete, I'm gonna have to get back with you on the details, but before I go, how far away from me were you sitting?"

"I figure about twenty or thirty feet at least."

"I've got the wrong kind of company at my door, and I need to grab a cap," I said quickly and hung up the phone then darted toward my bedroom for one of my Longhorn baseball caps. By the time I got back to the door, Dunbar was all frowns.

"I realize that this isn't the best of times, but Katrina Bible, a.k.a. Kat, was found dead about eight o'clock this morning in a room at the Highway Inn," Dunbar stated, looking over me with a high level of curiosity.

"What? Some trick went bad or something?" I asked while trying to remember where or if the photo album and Kat's letter was in Dunbar's eyesight. Normally, I would have invited the guy in, but I couldn't afford to let him spot that letter.

"A trick? Try a heroin overdose for size," he replied.

"Was it natural or sloppy like Hope's?"

"Door was locked from the inside, and it was intentionally done. You normally wear a ball cap around the house?" Dunbar asked curiously.

"Its part of my mojo, Detective."

"If I even had one person who would state that they saw a silhouette of your ass in that house or as much as in a two-block radius, I would haul your ass to jail."

"I don't have a clue as to what you're trying to imply, Detective, and by the way, it's Monday. Are we doing this solo, or am I a part of the team?" I asked.

He stared at me for about five seconds before responding. "You run by me and me alone because I'm not about to put my ass on the line for a hardheaded paperboy. Now for starters, what happened?" he asked about last night's events and pointed to my head.

"Someone was there before I showed up and had already been in the house because the back door was already unlocked, and the door leading into the house was wide open. I was hit from behind and didn't see who it was. So whatever they came for, they got it!"

"You have any idea who?" Dunbar asked.

"If I did, I would be on it by now, you think!" I stated sarcastically.

"Get you some rest because if someone steps up to pick up Kathy's body and make funeral arrangements, I'll need you there."

"You mean to tell me you're not planting one of your boys on watch?" I asked and again was sarcastic.

"You and I both know that oil and water don't mix," he said as he walked back to his car and drove off.

As soon as he backed out of the driveway, I went looking for the photo album. I flipped each page, looking for some kind of clue, but things weren't hitting for me. One thing that was tapping on my swollen noggin besides the massive headache was "heroin overdose." I wasn't classified as a street person, but I had to find out if this was a common outlet.

I grabbed my keys and drove to the *Herald*. As I approached the security desk in the lobby, I had to see if Peterson was on top of his game and if he took me seriously. I should have a temporary pass to come and go as I pleased throughout the building. "Can I help you, sir?" asked the security guard.

"Yeah, do you have a package for Trey Allen?"

"You have some identification, sir?" As soon as I presented my driver's license, he handed me a package.

Inside were a temporary employee tag, a pager, and a set of keys to a locker in the men's dressing room. I clipped my badge on my collar and took the elevator up. I arrived at the *Herald* when everybody was scrambling to get their columns in. Presses were being prepped, and I knew better than to bother any editor during these hours because they weren't themselves.

I jumped on the first empty computer that wasn't being used and started my search for anything remotely close to a pattern of death by overdose. Each time I ran into a past record that was supposedly being kept by this Jerry Bolder dude who just so happened to write the article on Hope, things just didn't look right. I'm sure Blacks and Hispanics weren't the only people using or shooting heroin or cocaine and dying from this shit.

"Bullshit!" I jumped on the phone to call the administration offices of the two hospitals in Waco for an accurate number on this body count. It didn't surprise me to know that such information didn't have to pass through the filter or was considered before it was given out. After explaining who I was and what I wanted the stats for, which turned out to be a white lie, I was patched in to the person that could help out.

"Morgue. This is Calvin."

"Calvin, this is Trey Allen from the *Waco Herald*, and I need your help on some information you have stored in your records."

"That's really going to depend on what you may be asking for, sir, because a lot of our files and information are classified by way of hospital policies."

"What I need won't get you in any boiling water, my good man," I said, reassuring him.

"Let me be the judge on that, sir. So what is it that you need, Trey?"

"Heroin overdoses in the last ten years by African-Americans, and if I'm still within the legal realm, I need names of only the females, please."

"Can I call you back? It's going to take me more than a few minutes to gather the information."

"I'm at extension 334," I stated as we ended our conservation.

I then called the second hospital and requested the same from them and was also asked for an allotted time. I had no intentions on moving one step, so I sat absolutely still in the chair I occupied and stayed out of everybody's way. As I sat there, I noticed a picture of two beautiful ladies sitting beside each other, and judging from the resemblance, it was mother and daughter. You could tell the little girl took center stage in who I now know as Michelle Evans, according to the plaques that were hanging from the walls of her tiny cubicle.

I couldn't help but to pick up a five-by-seven photo of her daughter that was in a sterling silver frame. She couldn't have been more than five and was gracefully poised just like her mother. My being who I am and doing the work that I do, I quickly noticed that Michelle didn't have a husband or was at least a single parent because there was no sign of this little girl's father or a man around for that matter.

Staring at the little girl got me to thinking about Darius and his condition. I was drawn back to the chaos on the floor of the *Herald* by a soft-spoken voice.

"She's beautiful, isn't she?"

"Excuse me," I said as I turned to see who the lady was.

"The little girl, she's beautiful, isn't she?" Michelle asked, pointing down at the picture of her daughter I held in my hand.

"Yes, she is," I replied as I handed her the framed picture of her daughter and slowly got out of her chair.

"You make it a habit of invading people's spaces?" she asked. She placed the picture back down on her desk.

"I didn't mean to, and I apologize if I offended you."

"Her name is Samantha. She would have been eight years old, a month and a half ago. She died of a rare kidney disease four years ago, and no matter how much times goes by, I miss her being around."

"I'm sorry to hear that. Judging by the picture, she was full of life," I stated and sparked a laugh from Michelle.

"And very silly too!" she revealed with a smile on her face.

I told her that she was a very strong lady, and she responded, "I only see this one way, Trey Allen. If my baby was that 'one in a thousand,' then God thought she was that special and wanted her back."

"Well, from what I know about her mother these past four minutes, she's telling the rest of heaven how special her mother is too."

"So what brought you to my desk?"

That question brought about fifty responses that I wanted to give her on a fly tip, but I wasn't going to go there.

"I guess it was out of everybody's way," I said in a way that gave her a clear indication that I was reaching for straws.

"Please don't tell me you're nervous, Trey Allen," she said as she crossed her arms across her chest and stood back on her legs.

"No, I'm not, but I'm try'n not to say something silly."

"Would that have made you more comfortable?" she asked with a smile on her face.

"Yeah, it would have, but as a man I have to distinguish when it is the appropriate time to be silly, and I'm not good at that right now."

"So, Mr. Trey Allen, what brought you to my cubicle?" she asked again with the anticipation that I would be myself. From what I was feeling within, the only response I could give her was *God!*

"How would you know something like that, Trey Allen?"

I was just about to spill my crush all over her blouse when her phone rang.

"Michelle Evans speaking," she glanced my way and handed me the phone, pulled open a drawer, gave me a pen, some paper, and walked away. It was hard determining whether or not she was coming back because she had her purse on her shoulder. "How did you know my name?"

She looked back at me and kept on walking.

"Trey Allen speaking."

"Calvin here. You ready for this?" he asked. "Gloria Cooper, Carla Web, Stephaney Sloan, Rebecca Green, Cheri Nolan, Angela Jones, Denise Ray, Mary Johnson, and Britney Webb. That's the best that I can do for you, Trey."

"Thank you, Calvin," I said as I rushed off the phone to pick up another line on Michelle's phone.

"Trey Allen speaking."

"Mr. Allen, this is Greg from the morgue. You ready?"

"Let's have 'em," I replied.

"Debra Long, Barbara Green, Jean Bell, Iola Frisk, Dee Dee Cotton, Andrea Freeman, Lisa Brown, and Sara Williams."

"I owe you one, Greg."

"Not a problem, Trey," he stated as he hung up.

I went ahead and added Kat to my list and by her overdose being self-inflicted, my only question was why. Since I couldn't get past the bureaucracy of the shield, I had to count on Dunbar to get me what I needed, so I called him.

I asked for Detective Dunbar, told the person who answered I was Trey Allen, and was put on hold. After about fifteen seconds, Dunbar was asking me to hold on. It was apparent that he just laid the phone down on his desk, and from what I was hearing, someone was chewing his ass out about wasting department man-hours on dry-ass hunches that weren't paying off for him. I guess he was grasping at straws on this investigation.

"Trey, is this important?" he asked in a part-frustrated, part-wounded tone. "Let's not get personal, Detective. I'm tired of standing in the middle of the crossroad concerning my sister. So back off, white boy, and take a good look at the people that are trying to help you."

"My bad, Allen. I'm having one of those weeks. So what's on your mind?"

I gave Dunbar all the female names and asked him to see if the doors were locked from the inside. I wanted to know if the door was locked intentionally or if the victims all had some company before the dope was ever shot.

"Give me an hour, Allen, because I have to go downstairs to kiss a little ass just to get this lady to drop what she's doing to help me."

"I'll be here at the *Herald*."

As I hung up the phone, I saw Peterson waiving me toward his office. I couldn't tell whether the frustration that was written all over his face was about his deadline or his lack of sleep.

"What's up, Pete?"

"Have a seat at my desk, and pick up line two. It's your aunt Vera."

"Aunt Vera, what's wrong?"

"Trey, this baby woke up crying out of his sleep and clinging onto me as if the devil was after him. I just got him to calm down."

I knew I shouldn't have let him to see his mama that way. Damn! "Is he all right now?" I asked.

"The boy's been asking about you for an hour, off and on, but he's okay." I told my aunty I would be there in about two hours.

Before I ended the conversation with Aunt Vera, Pete slid me a piece of paper with the name "Dr. Mona Sanchez" and in parenthesis was "Child psychologist. Call before you leave this office if you love Darius."

There wasn't a period of thought. I just dialed the number.

"Dr. Mona Sanchez's office. This is Sandra. How can I help you?"

"Sandra, my name is Trey Allen, and my nephew is having some problems that may need some attention. So I would like to speak with Dr. Sanchez, please."

"She's just about to walk a client out if you'd like to hold, Mr. Allen." I held. I started thinking about what he might have seen or gone through that night and up to noon the following day. Here I am thinking that or at least hoping that this whole ordeal wasn't affecting him because he wasn't going through any changes. That might not have been the case subconsciously though.

"Mr. Allen. I've been in this business for thirty years, and I can just about set my watch by the time these little people will start experiencing or going through some changes. From seeing that child on the news section, I gave him another week before he started to unravel. So what are his symptoms?" she asked.

"I guess I can count on Peterson to take care of me," I told her. With everything she had just said, I knew Pete had time to consult with her before I called.

"Peterson said he owed you one for accepting a position under him, and now he owes me one. Because I love helping these little people out, I would have bumped you past the paperwork without Peterson's favor. So let's get to Darius," she said.

"From what my aunt says, he woke up out of his sleep, crying."

"He's very afraid of something, and I assure you that whatever it is or whoever it is, it's on the surface of his subconscious, and sometime soon this thing or person will be his worst nightmare, Mr. Allen."

"Damn, Doc, did you have to say it like that?"

"Thirty years, Mr. Allen! I assure you that the next five to six days are going to be very hectic in whose ever home this child is in. So it's not going to make a big significance if you bring him in to see me or not right now because he has to let this thing or person come close to him in order for him to tell us who or what we're dealing with. If you want to help, don't coerce him by asking him or leading him to what you might think it is because that may hinder him from bringing whatever it is forward. Second, I would like to take him to lunch for a few days. That will be a quick way for me and him to establish some trust. The more relaxed he is with me, the more I can get out of him," she advised.

"You'll be feeding my aunt too."

She started laughing at my comment. "Please, forgive my outburst, but after finding out that Judge Evans granted custody to your aunt, I called her about ten minutes before you called me to get as much information as I could, and she suggested the lunches and wanted to come too."

"Since everybody is on top of everything, do I need to give you my aunt's number or have you already talked with her too?" I asked, trying not to sound too sarcastic. "I'll need that information from you, Mr. Allen," she said with a light chuckle.

As soon as I got off the phone with Dr. Sanchez, Pete walked back in and threw himself down on the sofa in his office. He placed a pillow over his face and said, "Seventeen years in this place, Trey."

"Are you in need of a hug, Pete?"

"No! What I need is a hungry journalist that won't give up. I thank God I don't have any competition to deal with, but I try to run this place as if I do. You understand where I'm coming from, Allen?"

"Since you mentioned it. I was really trying to take a break from that, but the more I think about it, that's what really keeps us going in this business. Isn't it?" I asked him as he sat up.

"Bravo!" he said as he slowly clapped his hands a few times. "Damn! Before I get caught in the moment, get your ass out of my chair, find a desk somewhere in the building that's not being used, and call Detective Dunbar. All he said was 'You're going to like sunken treasure.'"

That was an indication that he found something. "Pete, thank you for the referral!"

"Listen, if you can't get past this case and everything surrounding it, then I can't get a hundred percent out of you, and if I can't get a hundred, you're not Trey Allen. So go find you a desk and call Dunbar back."

Though Pete sounded like he had some rough edges, I knew he was smiling inside.

I saw Michelle sitting at her desk and since she had no problem with me being myself, I was going to be just that! I snatched a chair from an unoccupied station and rolled it up to her desk. She saw me coming and from the look she had on her face, she was clearly saying, "Ohh no you're not!"

I positioned my chair in a way that she couldn't get out or get past me. "Trey, what are you doing?" she asked me with a frown on her face.

"I was told to find me a desk, and since God brought me to this one the first time, I figured he wouldn't mind if I came back. With you being so damn rude toward me, I was tempting to turn my heels, but

I'm a strong believer in predestination. How about you?" I asked her as I reached over to grab a pad and took a pen out of her hand.

"I'm being rude? What do you call what you're doing? And give me back my pen," she demanded. She snatched her pen out of my hand.

"So what am I'm going to write with now, Michelle?" I asked as I dialed up Dunbar.

"For starters, you need to get your ass out of my cubicle, and second, stop messing with things that don't belong to you," she requested, and for emphasis, she placed her hands on her hips.

"Detective Dunbar, please." Michelle and I stared at each other. "Just rude," I said jokingly. I reached over and turned a picture of her daughter toward me. "Please tell God that your mother is being rude to me, Samantha."

Michelle slapped me on my shoulder. "You leave her out of this," she said and moved Samantha's picture away from me. "You were rude because you walked away and never gave me the opportunity to answer your question, and now you're sitting here, assaulting me."

"Since I'm on the line with the police, I ought to turn your ass in for abuse."

"No, you didn't," she stated as she tossed the pen down in front of me.

"Don't be nice now, toughy!" I gave her the pen and the paper back.

"Trey, hold on to your hat. Carla Web . . ." I told Dunbar to hold on so I could place the pen in Michelle's hand, slide the pad to her, and began to call out the first name Dunbar gave me as I tapped on the pad.

She began to write, biting down on her bottom lip. "We're going to fight after this," she whispered as she wrote the names down.

"Cheri Nolan, Mary Johnson, Barbara Green, and Andre Freeman filed charges on Donald 'Spoon' Simms but never followed through on the matter. Get this, though, Carla, Mary, and Barbara were found with too much dope in their system and a clean vial, no drawback.

"So I'm assuming that they did the first shot, nodded like they do after a fresh hit, and someone gave them another straight dose before they could even know what was going on. Overdose, suicide, or murder?" Dunbar asked.

"Murder!" I replied. "I'm going to start a probe within my own station that just might land me into some more hot water, but shit like this you just don't let go!"

As I ended my conversation with Dunbar, my thoughts of him wanting to find out why those girls' deaths weren't ruled as a murder let me know that he was about to come face-to-face with a dangerous dragon—one that has been terrorizing my people for hundreds of years. For a white boy to question the morals, principles, and how his own kind chose to deal with a nigga was a violation.

I didn't have to ask if the girls on my list were black or not, but it didn't stop me from wanting to know why. For Dunbar to question why, meant that he wanted to know who and why top officials allowed them to get swept under the rug or discarded like some common trash. This was the same dragon that I faced in the beginning of my career, and I chose to stand firm. But if Dunbar did what I did, it meant he would be questioning the integrity of the chief of his department.

"I need to know where they keep the past issues on microfilm, and I need you to help me do some research, Michelle," I said with a broken spirit as I held a picture of Samantha in my hand. Michelle heard the confusion in my voice.

"Trey, I can't push my responsibilities aside to help you."

"What is it that you do anyway?" I asked.

"I oversee typesetting."

"So don't you have assistants to help you?" I asked.

"What does that have to do with my job, Trey?"

I jumped on the phone to call Pete. "Pete, I just got off the phone with Dunbar. I'm on to something right now, and I need some help."

"What do you need?" he asked.

"Michelle Evans!"

"What? Trey, she's my backbone in that department." We both got quiet, and I felt him looking out of his office window at me.

I stood up and stared back at him as I waited on his response.

"Damn it, Trey! I want her back on her own field in seventy-two hours, and if you haven't found what you're looking for by then, you're shit out of luck."

"Thank you, Pete."

Michelle looked up at Pete as he continued to stare down on us. "Get your assistant on the line, you'll be with me for the next three days," I informed her as I placed her purse strap across her shoulder and pushed the phone in front of her.

I could tell that Michelle still wanted to uncap her true thoughts from the frowns over her eyebrows.

"Why don't you just say what you want to say, Michelle?" She stopped dead in her tracks, placed one hand on her hip, and the other index finger pointed toward my chest.

"Let's get one thing straight. I am not rude, and I don't appreciate you pulling me away from my job. You don't know me for one, and I don't like or appreciate you handling me like this either."

I could see untold stories lurking behind Michelle's beauty. There was a sudden look in her eyes that portrayed rough times, I was figuring with whatever his name was. I could tell that whatever I did to trigger the anger was going to remain a secret within her.

"Michelle," I said gently as I slowly lowered her hand away from my chest.

"You miss her a lot, don't you?" She stared at me with tears in her eyes. I felt her hand begin to tremble and knew that she was about to break down any moment. "Come on, woman," I said as I led her out of the *Herald* and down to my car. Once she was seated in the passenger seat and I shut her door, the tears spilled over her eyelids—with fury.

As I walked around to the driver's side of the car, we both stared into each other's faces, and when I got into the car, I knew not to try to hug her. I just drove off the lot and let her to do her thing. She told me she cried every day, and from the way she started in on me, obviously, he didn't show her the affection she needed.

I waited until she had emptied her tears. "What's his name?" She glanced over at me as she continued to clean her face up.

"First name Heartless, last name Piece of Shit!" she said bluntly.

"I won't apologize for his actions and I don't know him either, but we both know that he loved Samantha very much. It's evident that he couldn't deal with the emotional state her death caused and found his own corner to retreat to in order to deal with this. If you ask me, he still loves you."

"If he did, he never would have walked away, and I didn't ask you."

"No, you didn't ask me, and no, I don't know you, but I want to, Michelle. You mentioned God earlier. Do you trust him?"

"Trey, what kind of question is that?"

"It's a logical question, Michelle. For all I know, you could be hating God for taking Samantha away from you and trying to convince yourself that the comment you made earlier was the one you wanted to accept."

"I struggled for three years to have a baby, and when I did get pregnant, she was stripped away from me. Hell, I can't have any more children, so yes, I'm upset, Trey."

"Do you trust him or not, Michelle?"

"I don't know, Trey!" she shouted and began to sob.

"Well, I do. I don't do a lot of praying, and I haven't found the urge to attend church since my parents passed away, but I trust him. I'm not going to ever tell you to let your daughter go, and for whatever reason, God won't allow you to have any more children. You were blessed to have a child who really loved you, and for that, you should be thankful."

"What makes you think that I'm not?" she asked.

"I'm not questioning that, Michelle. Do you hate men that much that you won't allow me or any other man close to you?"

"I'm doing fine all by myself," she replied. "You're full of shit, and we both know that." She quickly popped me on my shoulder.

"Are you going to keep beating me up?" I asked her.

She never responded.

"You have two minutes to pull yourself together, bully." I was less than a half a mile from Aunt Vera's.

"Where are we going? Or, should I say, where are you taking me?"

"I'm taking you to meet Darius."

"Who's Darius?"

"The seventeen-month-old boy whose mom was murdered about ten days ago."

"The baby that was on the news?" she asked surprisingly.

"He's my nephew, and Hope was his mother. He's having to deal with some issues in his little life that we as adults can't understand yet. We all need some love, Michelle. It's just a matter of whether you're willing to accept it when something genuine comes your way."

She stared at me. "So what are you trying to say, Trey Allen?" she asked.

"You're a woman, Michelle. I don't have to tell you anything," I stated as I pulled into Aunt Vera's driveway. Darius was playing in the front yard when we drove up. As soon as Michelle saw Darius and Darius saw her, they both stared frozen in time and just looked at each other.

I was sure once Darius saw me he would come running, but Michelle had his attention. She finally got out of the car and slowly walked over to Darius and picked him up. From where Aunt Vera and I were standing on the porch, we couldn't hear what Michelle was saying to Darius. But shortly afterward, he hugged her neck as if she were Hope, in the flesh.

I gave Aunt Vera a kiss on her cheek before going in the house to answer the phone. After hearing Dunbar's voice on the phone, I started to wonder if I were being followed. "Damn, Dunbar. You got a tail on me?"

"Stop bullshitin', Trey. Peterson said you might be headed to your aunt's, but listen to this. Your girl Katrina was a suspect in two of the cases, but the investigating officer didn't have enough to push for an indictment on either case."

"So was Spoon a suspect or questioned at either time?" I asked.

"Cleared on both," he said.

"You think Kat might have had some hidden agenda because Hope drew Spoon out of the streets?" I asked.

"The good folks at Mt. Zion Hill Baptist Church can view Donald Simms as a religious success story, but the Feds were two seconds away from arresting his ass. One thing I do know. Every girl that was under him has slumped real low and still won't roll on him to save their lives. So who knows what Katrina was holding on to?"

"So where do we go from here?" I asked Dunbar to see exactly where his heart was.

"I want to know why the deaths of these girls weren't ruled as murders and treated as such. The fact that Simms is in the core, I have a right to ask without getting my ass chewed off for worrying about something that doesn't pertain to this case."

"I've got to go, Dunbar," I quickly said as I saw a gray Cadillac pull behind my car.

By the time I got out on the front porch, Aunt Vera was shaking Judge Evans's hand. It was then apparent to me that she stood on her word about stopping by to see Darius. There was something about Michelle and Judge Evans, and it snapped as I looked at their postures. Surely the judge couldn't be her mother?

"Mr. Allen, you seem to be a magnet amongst my family, or this really is a small world," Judge Evans stated as she took Darius out of Michelle's arms.

On that note, I walked down to where the four ladies were because I knew I was about to find out what I wanted to know.

"Trey, this is my aunt Gwendolyn and her best friend, Dr. Mona Sanchez," Michelle said with a sense of pride.

"I'll make it a habit to ask any other female that I might come in contact with if she's already acquainted with you all because this is very creepy," I stated before shaking the judge's and Dr. Sanchez's hand. They all found some humor in my comment, but I was dead serious.

Darius and I looked at each other, and the ladies saw the connection between us.

"You okay, nephew?" I really wanted to know if he could tell me that he was going to be all right, but him leaning over toward me to squeeze my nose was good enough for me. I couldn't help taking two steps toward him to kiss his forehead.

I was hoping like hell Dr. Sanchez wasn't right about him going through the shit she mentioned.

"So where are you all headed, if you don't mind me asking?" I directed my question toward Dr. Sanchez.

"Chuck E. Cheese, of course. Kids love the place. To be straight with you, I'm feeding him to make sure he's good and tired before we get back to my office. I've got a big couch he can nap on. If his experiences are close encounters, I'll be there to find out what I can do to help him get past this. It's torture on a child to have to keep going through such a thing for long periods of time."

"Uncle Trey," I said to Darius, and he pointed at me and smiled. "That's right, buddy. Whenever you need me, little man," I said as I gently pinched his nose. I hated to break the gathering up, but Michelle and I had some work to do.

"Mr. Allen, you take care of my niece," stated Judge Evans.

"She has no plans of letting me to do any such a thing, Judge. In fact, I'm thinking about pressing assault charges against her." Just as I said that, she popped me on the arm. "Can I get her indicted for that?" I asked jokingly.

"Well, if you ask me, that was more of a love lick," Judge Evans stated.

"Aunt Gwen, you need to stop," Michelle interrupted quickly as she placed her hands on her hips.

"Girl, I'm a judge. It's my job to judge things. Mona, what's your diagnosis?"

"Clinically, girl, a love lick to me too!" Dr. Sanchez said as they gave each other a high five.

"I am so through messing with the both of you. Ms. Jenkins, you have a nice day, and please don't let any of them rub off on you," Michelle said to my aunt.

"Child, I've been around Trey all his life, and the way he's looking at you, you might as well start pick'n out your wedding dress."

"Are you just going to stand there and let them get away with this?" Michelle asked me.

"I'm not mad at either one of them," I whispered to her as I got in the car. Michelle held a schoolgirl smirk on her face as we drove back to the *Herald*.

"So what's on your mind, Michelle?"

"You're willing to put up with my emotional state?"

"No, but I am willing to help you get past it."

"Isn't that the same thing?" she asked.

"No! You haven't moved beyond a lot of things, and I'm not willing to take his place if you're asking or referring to a courtship."

"Am I that bad off, Trey?"

"Yeah, Michelle, you are!" She remained quiet for a few minutes, but I didn't want the conversation to end.

"So are you going to send me a little note to wherever my desk is going to be, asking me if I'll be your boyfriend?"

"What! Trey, I've known you for a few hours."

"So you don't think these last few hours are special?"

"Do you?" she asked.

"Look at it this way, lady. I don't, and I'm not willing to start our acquaintance over, and since the man upstairs saw that it was the way this was supposed to go, then this is normal enough for me. Do you have a problem with his way of doing things?" I asked her.

"No, I don't, Trey."

"Then kiss me on my cheek if you want me to be in your life until death do us part."

"Now that sounds like a proposal to me," she said.

"Take it any way you want because I'm done talking." I didn't push the issue any further. Hell, I thought a few hours was short, but I wanted her and all her baggage.

"The names of these females you wrote down, they were murdered, I think. No, forget that. I know that their deaths were swept under the rug because they were black and prostitutes."

"You can't be serious," Michelle said as she dug in her purse for the list.

"I'm not willing to use Hope as an example to prove my point to you and to show you how Waco feels about an ex-pimp's girlfriend."

"Are you saying Hope was a prostitute, Trey?"

"Hell no! She was just his straight-up girlfriend. Detective Dunbar is a white boy who understands one thing—to do what he was trained to do. I overheard him getting his ass chewed on because he was wasting too many man-hours on hunches."

"If he gives up trying to find out who murdered my sister, his supervisors won't say a damn word."

"I think you're wrong, Trey. I've been working at the *Herald* for a while, and with all the crazy stuff that happens in this city, the police crew pretty much solves their cases."

"I'm glad you said that and feel that way. I want you to start with the murder of the McAllen boy whose arms were tied behind his back with some rope and placed, faced forward, in an old refrigerator fifteen years ago just outside the city. What young boy would tie himself up, walk face first into a refrigerator, and close the damn door behind him, knowing that it had a latch on it, and he wasn't going to be able to get out? Cold case or closed case, Michelle?"

"We'll see, Trey!"

"Oh come on, Michelle! This is the age of technology, and this DNA shit is solving a lot of unsolved crimes. Do you think the evidence in that boy's case has been tested? What about the evidence in those girls' cases?" I was upset and refused to put on blinders.

"Put your hand on the back of my head." She was hesitant to do so. "Do it, Michelle!"

She felt the knot and frowned.

"I was sneaking into my parents' home to take a look around, and somebody hit me in the head with a metal object. Whoever it was went there to get something that would give them up as the murderer. Waco CSI crew went in twice and came up empty. They didn't give it their best shot, Michelle. They didn't go all out because she was black."

"Are you about to turn this into a racial issue, Trey?"

"Hell, I don't have to! I want a list of murders that hit the pages of the *Herald*. I want the racial count. I want the count on the solved and unsolved for the past twenty years and find out who the next of kin are to the ladies on your list too."

"So what are you going to be doing while I'm doing all of this?" she asked as I parked in the lot of the *Herald*.

"Finding us a bigger working space. You're getting out of that corner, or cave, shall I say."

"I like my space just fine, Trey."

"You do realize that Pete is my friend?" I asked her.

"And what?" she asked in an all-out ghetto style.

"Where I go, you go! So since your cubicle is too small for the both of us, it's time to upgrade."

I didn't give her room to say another word. I just got out of the car and walked into the *Herald* without looking back at her. I didn't hear her car door shut, so I knew she was sitting in the car thinking about God knows what.

SHOW-AND-TELL

Five hours after we left Aunt Vera's, I had found three times the amount of space that I was looking for, but to keep tempers from flaring up behind the new guy stepping over some imaginary seniority lines, I made arrangements to move Michelle and me out of her cave later on that night.

As I was walking around, scavenging for things that weren't being used, I heard a whistle coming from the second-floor level. Pete was trying to get my attention. As I looked his way, he dropped a piece of paper to the first floor. I walked over to pick it up, and all it had on it was an address. "Dr. Sanchez wants you at her office immediately," he said.

Damn! Darius! I ran toward the front door. Whatever it was, it couldn't be good because I would be on the phone talking about it. It was thirty minutes before I reached her office, and as I walked into the lobby, I could hear Darius crying from a distance.

There was no need to ask for directions to her office. I just followed the sounds of Darius's cry. Walking into her office, Aunt Vera was rocking him. As soon as he saw me, he scrambled out of her lap and ran toward me as fast as his little legs could carry him. I scooped him up, and we wrapped our arms around each other. "Bad thing. Bad, Trey," he said, continuing to cry.

"I got you, little man. Let's get out of here," I told him as I carried him out the door. Aunt Vera was bringing up the rear without hesitation.

I left Dr. Sanchez and Judge Evans standing in the office. They both knew that there was nothing to talk about. Whatever happened, I would eventually hear about it before the day was over.

Darius calmed down before we made it to the house. He had already figured out that sleep was his worst enemy, and from what I was seeing, he was fighting to stay away from that realm as best he could. I knew one thing was for sure; sleep was going to take him soon. No matter how much he fought it, he was going to lose, and there was nothing I could do about it!

I carried Darius in the house, both of us taking to the couch. I grabbed the remote and turned on the television in search for a cartoon or something I thought he would enjoy watching. As I flipped through the channels, the only thing I thought would be cool enough for him was a documentary on the African nation.

I seriously thought about flipping through the photo album with him that Kat sent me but was hesitant to do so because not seeing Hope could be his problem. The more I stared at the photo album lying two feet away from me on the coffee table, the more I was inclined to test the waters. If doing an elimination of things could help me help him, then I had to start somewhere.

Propping him up on my lap, I reached over and grabbed the damn thing. Just as I closed my eyes and took a couple of deep breaths before opening the photo album, I heard Michelle's voice.

"Are you praying or concentrating on something?" she asked. I looked, and she was standing in the doorway of the living room.

"Damn, girl! You scared me." Darius found some humor in how I reacted to her spooking me the way she did, and he laughed.

"For the record, my aunt Gwen likes you, and thought I should stop by to check on the two of you."

"What does that have to do with the way you feel?" I asked as I opened the photo album to the first set of photos.

"I brought Darius some crayons and a coloring book," she said, avoiding the question. Darius accepted the gifts and smiled up at me.

"Tell her thank you, Darius." He gripped the coloring book and colors with a bear hug and laid his head on my chest.

"Would you like to sit down or do you have to run off?" I asked Michelle.

"I was wondering when your manners were going to kick in!" she said dryly and sat a few inches to the left of me and Darius.

"Mama, Trey," Darius said when he saw Hope in a picture.

"Mama, Mama, Mama, Mama," he said as he pointed at every picture Hope was in.

"Who is this, Darius?" I asked him, pointing at Kat.

"Mama," he ignored me, and he took his own index finger and pointed at Hope.

"Okay, I see you can recognize your mother, but what about her?" I asked again and pointed at another picture of Kat holding him. It was evident that Hope took the picture of them that day. He just continued to point out Hope wherever he saw her.

That ended with "Mama get it, Trey," and his pointing at a picture of him sitting on the floor in the living room.

"Yeah, that's Mama, Darius," I replied.

"That is not what he is saying, Trey," Michelle said as she stopped me on the next page.

Darius saw the picture of him sitting in the living room floor again. "Mama get it, Trey. Mama get it," he repeated while he pointed at a blanket he was sitting on.

I looked at Michelle for a second and started flipping and scanning every set of photographs until I saw the blanket again. Michelle and I looked at each other, anticipating Darius saying it again. I guess it took him a minute to spot the blanket in the second photo.

After pointing out his mother four times, he spotted the blanket. "Mama take it, Trey," he said again and again, pointing to the blanket that was lying across the arm of the sofa. Again I flipped through the remaining pages and scanned the rest of the pictures for a shot of the blanket. I saw it again on the last page of the photo album.

It was a picture of Darius sleeping, and the same blanket was covering him as he slept.

"Mama take it," he said again. Then he slapped at the picture negatively. It was evident that he liked the blanket, so I made it my business to talk to Dunbar about going to my parents' house to retrieve the blanket. Hell, it might ease some things on his mind.

The roar of a lion on the television caught Darius's attention, and once Darius got a good fix on the lion, he went ballistic!

"Bad, Uncle Trey. Bad, bad, bad, Trey." He shouted, crying and pointing to the lion. Michelle quickly reached for the remote and turned the television off. With Darius crying the way he was, Aunt Vera came racing into the room.

"Bad, Uncle Trey," he said again as he continued to cry.

"It's okay, nephew, it's off now," I reassured him. I had to turn him to make him see that the TV was off.

"Bad, Uncle Trey."

"Okay, buddy. I got you now." I really didn't have the slightest clue as to what he wanted me to know, but it upset me that his little world was all shook-up, and I couldn't fix it!

Eventually he cried himself to sleep, and I sat by his side as he slept. I didn't want him to wake up terrified of this bad thing that haunted him in his sleep and now while he was awake.

Dr. Sanchez's conversation was replaying over and over in my mind, and I was coming face-to-face with Darius, growing closer to whatever it was that was terrorizing him.

I guess fatigue must have set in on me and surprisingly Michelle too! It was right after midnight, and she was reclined in the La-Z-Boy with a blanket laid over her too. I quietly slipped into the kitchen to pick up some food in case Darius woke up running from this thing.

"She talked in her sleep."

"Damn it, Aunt Vera, stop creepin' up on me like that!" I said. I almost dropped the plate out of my hand.

I gathered she was talking about Michelle. "Everybody talks in their sleep, Aunt Vera."

"Not like this, Trey." Aunt Vera made it sound as if it was some wicked shit was going on with Michelle. Being a graduate from nosy university, I didn't have to ask her again. Aunt Vera was going to tell me anyway.

"Who is Samantha?" she asked. The question really shook me off my axle, and I really needed to hear this. I knew Michelle was still trying to deal with the loss of Samantha, but if this was going to be some multiple personality stuff, I was going to have to have a serious conversation with her.

"Never seen or heard nothing like it, Trey."

"Samantha is her daughter. She died four years ago when she was four."

"As sure as there is a God above, her child is as close to that woman as you are to that chicken on your plate."

"Okay, Aunt Vera, you sounding kinda spooky right now."

"You can call it what you want, boy, but it ain't a bad thing to her, I guess. Me not ever having a child of my own, I wouldn't know the depths of pain when it comes to losing a child."

"It's a very heartfelt situation that a mother has to deal with all her life," Michelle whispered from the doorway of the kitchen.

"All right, that's it! The next time either one of you tips up on me like this again, I'm going off!" I said, rather loud.

"Trey, lower your voice before you wake that baby," Aunt Vera insisted.

"Too late. He's already up, and you need to come see this," Michelle said with a cold glare. She stepped back out of the entryway of the kitchen to give me passing room.

I stared at her for a cool five seconds. Aunt Vera and I looked at each other for a second, and I slowly placed the piece of chicken I was eating down on my plate.

"Michelle, are you okay?" I asked her with an uneasy feeling.

"Trey, don't trip and I'll explain later, but you have to come and see this," she said as she extended her hand out to me.

Taking her hand, I let her lead me back into the den with Aunt Vera in tow. Aunt Vera reached the den before I did, and I heard her saying, "Never seen or heard nothing like it, Trey."

Darius was coloring in the coloring book when we walked in. He looked up from his work with a chilling stare on his little face that made me take a step back. "Darius, come here, little man," I said. I squatted down and held my arms out to receive him. He never took his eyes off me and never blinked.

This shit really had me in the twilight zone. "Darius, come here, nephew," I said to him again.

"Bad, Uncle Trey. It bad, bad, bad, bad, Trey," he kept repeating, walking toward me with his drawn artwork in his hand. Just as he began to put his arms around my neck, I gently removed the picture of a lion he colored from his hand. "Bad, Uncle Trey," he said. After that, he hugged my neck real tight.

I stood back up with Darius in my arms and stared at the picture with confusion. "Yeah, Darius, this thing is real bad, nephew." The only coloring that he did on the whole picture was on the eyes of the lion. He still had the red crayon in his hand, and he had colored the eyes of this lion so heavily that the crayon was halfway used up.

"Darius, look at Uncle Trey." He looked me in the face in despair. "Darius, is this the bad thing?"

"Bad, Uncle Trey. Bad, bad." He then slapped his hand at it.

I kissed him on his cheek and handed him to Aunt Vera. She took him to her room and laid him in her bed. Michelle and I just stood there looking at one another. I was at a crossroads with this lion and its red eyes, and I was trippin' on Michelle because she and I both knew that she wasn't coming clean with me on something.

"Are you going to talk to me or what?" I asked her, taking her hand and holding it.

"Trey, how am I supposed to talk to you about something that I don't understand myself? I'm afraid at times. I think I'm going insane. I'm embarrassed and totally insecure," she admitted, her head hung low.

I pulled her into my arms and hugged her. "Two days, Michelle, and you're standing in my aunt's house at one thirty in the morning in my arms. Is this normal to you?"

"No!" she replied.

"Then why are you here, Michelle?"

"Trey, don't do this, please," she whispered.

"Why, Michelle?"

"She talked to me, Trey." She held her head up and looked at me directly.

"Is that why you brought the coloring book and turned the television off when he saw the lion?"

"Yes."

"This is the part of you that your husband couldn't take."

"I'm not crazy, Trey," she said as she tried to dislodge herself from me.

"It's not that easy with me, Michelle, because I don't want to get away from you," I said as I pulled her back into my arms. "How did she know?"

"I picked him up in the yard yesterday. I went home to get some sleep, and she told me what his fears were. What it means, I don't know and neither does she, so don't push me." Her head dropped again.

"I don't have to tell you that you talk in your sleep, do I?" I asked her as I lifted her head to meet mine.

"No!"

"Can Samantha help us out in another way, Michelle?"

"She's slipping further and further away from me as my days pass. She comes and goes when she wants to and not on my request. She said you have to trust Darius."

"You're not setting foot on the streets tonight, so consider yourself a guest in this house. Come on, and I'll show you to your bedroom," I told her, pulling her by the hand.

"Are you always so demanding?"

"Only when I care. You got a problem with that?" We stood face-to-face within inches of each other.

"Don't take it personally, but you need some mouthwash. Can I go lie down?" she said as she stared into my eyes.

"Not until you shower first!" I replied.

"Are you trying to insinuate that I'm musty or something, Trey?"

"No. I'm just infatuated with your perfume, and when you're gone and I'm lying in my bed alone, I want to get some sleep without torturing myself with your scent. So go shower!"

"How am I supposed to do that when you won't let me go? Where's the shower?"

I pointed down the hall and told her "last room on the right" and that my T-shirts were in the top drawer to her right. She smiled and asked, "And where will you be sleeping?"

"On the couch, of course."

As soon as I saw my bedroom door close behind Michelle, I went back into the den, removed one of the photographs with the blanket in it that Darius had pointed out of the photo album, and went to Aunt Vera's room. I was glad to see her bedroom door open and her still up.

"Every time I look up you're reading that Bible."

"This is how your aunty finds her peace, child. You'll come around one day, baby, trust me," she said.

I walked up to her and knelt down beside her bed and kissed her cheek. Putting the picture of Darius sleeping with his blanket in her face, I said, "Where is this blanket, Aunty?"

"Child, I haven't laid eyes on that blanket in about three weeks."

"I've gotta go do some work, Aunty. I hope you don't mind, but I'm making Michelle stay here until morning."

"You doing right, baby. A lady ain't got no business on the streets this time of the night."

I told her that I would be back before breakfast and left her to finish reading.

Before leaving the house, I called the police station and left a message for Dunbar to meet me at my parents' house. I hadn't really expected any uninvited company, but my rules didn't change about carrying my pistol.

For good reason, I was going to stay my ass out of the house this time. I sat outside of my parents' house over thirty minutes, waiting on Dunbar, and though I rehearsed my reason over twenty times for calling him out of bed, my wanting that blanket for Darius wasn't going to be good enough.

As he pulled up behind me, all I had was a hunch. I sure as hell couldn't tell him that I was looking for a fired-eyed lion either. With all the frowns on his face, I knew he wasn't in the mood for jokes either.

"Waking me out of my sleep—this better be good, Allen," he said as he placed his pistol in his shoulder holster.

"Sleep! I would have felt bad if you would have been sexin' the wife, but since you weren't doing a damn thing, I don't feel bad at all, brother. I need inside the house."

"You want to fill me in or what?" he stated before taking another step.

"You and your people went in looking for the unusual. It's my turn now, and I need to see the usual."

He looked at me for about five seconds and then started walking toward the door. As soon as he opened the door, the odor from the dried-up blood in the carpet attacked me and my senses.

This situation wasn't new to me, but as soon as the lights came on, I did all I could do not to show Dunbar that I was having an anxiety attack. All I could see was Hope lying lifeless on the floor, looking up at me and calling out my name.

"Allen, you have to breathe, dude," Dunbar said, placing his hand on my shoulder.

"I'm okay, man. I'm all right," I stated as I began to look around in the living room.

Something was wrong, and I just had to focus. Though Hope had put just a little twist in the decor, it was still Mama's touch. I turned full circle three times, frame by frame until it hit me.

"There's a trophy missing," I whispered.

"What's that?" Dunbar asked.

"A trophy, it's missing!" I blurted as I started to count them. "Killeen State Finals, 1981, with a gold medal hanging from a powder blue ribbon."

"You sure about that, Allen?" I turned around slowly to face him. I guess the look on my face said it all. "Okay, okay, my bad, brother. What half do you want?" Dunbar asked.

"Half of what?" I asked.

"Look, I got my ass chewed on the last time I called in for some help, and my insinuating that those black prostitutes weren't given priority treatment didn't go too well with my supervisors. So it's you and me."

"You take the bedrooms, I'll take this room, the den, and the kitchen. If the trophy is still here, let's find it. The medal on the light blue ribbon is at the station, so there's no need to look for it."

"So what are you going to do about the girls, Dunbar?"

"The right thing, Allen! I'm pushing to get the cases reopened and have them all ruled as a homicide."

I turned to walk toward the bedrooms with a smile on my face. I turned back around to give him the photo and said matter-of-factly, "By the way, I'm looking for this blanket."

"You woke me up for a freak'n blanket?"

"Nah, chump. I woke your ass up to tell you that a trophy was missing."

He smiled at me and threw his hands up.

It was after six in the morning before we met back up in the living room, and both of us were sweating like two hogs at the slaughterhouse. We stood there, breathing hard. "There's one way under the house, and no one has been under there because the paint around the seal hasn't been broken," Dunbar explained.

"I've had the ceiling area and the fireplace done twice, so if the killer wanted to hide the damn thing because he or she surely came back for it, where would they have hidden it, Trey?"

"Wherever it is, your team didn't find it, and I let this person get past me that night. Listen, I have to get back to my aunt's. I promised her that I would be back before breakfast, and I left a female friend with her."

"You mean Michelle Evans?" he asked with a smile on his face.

"How would you know something like that?" I asked.

"I called, looking for you, and I was directed to her. Before I could get off the phone, she had cornered me into providing her with some info on the list of women I gave you and the kid out of Bellmead. So I just figured it was her."

"So what did she find out?" I asked.

"Same shit I did. The department looked over their deaths," he replied.

"I'm going to be straight up with you, Dunbar. After this shit is over with, I'm writing a piece on the department that won't be too pretty. So if it takes me to expose such treatment toward my people, then that's what I'm going to do. If you want to stay clear, I'll understand it."

"How long did it take you to practice that bullshit? I'm a good detective without a color barrier. I want in, and I want my name in neon lights. Michelle has enough information to start a fire, and if you need some shit you can't have, push the brass in front of a camera to explain themselves, and that will force their hands. I figured if a conspiracy to get my badge comes along, I'll go into private investigating, but at least I'll go out knowing I did the right thing!"

We shook hands and left the house after straightening up a few things.

By the time I got back to Aunt Vera's, Michelle was gone. I smelled Aunt Vera stirring up some food, and as bad as I wanted to go straight in, take a shower, and sleep for about ten hours, I was SOL! It was nice walking in on Darius and not seeing him all shaken up.

"Michelle gone bye-bye, Uncle Trey" were the first words I heard after I closed the front door behind me.

"Yeah, I see you let her get away from me, but it's not your fault, nephew." I picked him up and gave him a hug.

"Michelle said that she wasn't about to let you see her in her just-waking-up stage. She is such a wonderful girl, Trey, and you need to start courtin' that girl before some other man steals her heart."

"First of all, Aunt Vera, courtin' is too country, and I've already asked the woman to marry me."

"Boy! You haven't known the woman a week. How do you expect her to agree to marry you in just four days of knowing you? Child, wait till I tell Jean about this."

"Aunt Vera, look at your nephew, and tell me what you see."

"I see a musty-ass nephew that needs to get out of my kitchen, go shower, come eat, and then I might just see another side of you," she said, chuckling.

"So we got jokes this morning, I see. She do any talking in her sleep?"

"I don't know, boy!" she stated in an evasive manner.

"Aunt Vera?"

"The door was shut. How was I supposed to know?"

I left her in the kitchen mumbling to herself as I passed Darius. He had yet another picture out of the coloring book that he was working on, and when I walked up on him, he was doing his thing in a way a kid his age should. "Hey, nephew! What are you working on?" He answered by pinching my nose.

"Is that bad too, Darius?" I asked as I pointed down at the zebra he was coloring on. He looked up at me and back down at the coloring book. Suddenly, he started flipping the pages in the book until he ran into a small picture of a lion at a water hole, and at some point that morning, he made it his objective to find every lion in the book and color their eyes red.

"Bad, Uncle Trey," he stated as he pointed at the lion.

I kissed him on the top of his head and turned the pages to his coloring book back to his zebra. He pointed at the zebra and said, "Horsey, Trey." I couldn't help but laugh and wonder if I was that nerdy when I was his age.

After showering and scarfing down some breakfast, I went to see Dr. Sanchez about Darius's flaming-eyed lion. I didn't want to crash in on her busy schedule, so I arrived before her doors opened. As she drove up, her facial expression told its own story, one with a heavy burden.

"You got a few minutes, Doc?" I asked before she could even kill the engine in her car. I handed her Darius's drawing, and she just looked back up at me.

She asked if this was Darius's, and I said that it was.

"He's getting closer, Mr. Allen. Michelle have anything to do with this?" She started to gather up her briefcase and files.

"What kind of question was that, Doc?"

"She couldn't come straight out and tell you because she didn't think you would understand, and she's tired of people thinking or calling her crazy."

"Yeah, she had a lot to do with it, and I don't think she's crazy."

"She's a good girl, Mr. Allen. She's my goddaughter, and I love her to death, so treat her right. Darius, pay attention to him, Mr. Allen. He's about to tell you why he's so scared of that lion," she said before she walked to her office.

I had missed out on arriving to the *Herald* to move my belongings into my new space. I was really trying not to be rude and just move Michelle out of her safety zone too quickly, but I had to talk her into moving her personal items into the spot I picked out for her when she was ready.

Seeing her car on the lot when I got there meant that she didn't waste any time getting on the job before I arrived. I was usually there before she arrived, and that had my curiosity flared up like a bad case of hemorrhoids.

I went up to see Pete before doing anything else and found the man stretched out on his couch. Well, let me rephrase that, his bed! I felt some compassion for the man, and so I just let him sleep. As soon as I noticed that he had the cord to his phone unplugged from the wall and wrapped around the phone, I knew he didn't want to be disturbed.

I saw Michelle going through her department, signing off on things, shaking hands with certain staff members, and doing her supervisory thing. I couldn't help but notice that she had stepped up her attire to a navy blue, two-piece blazer and skirt set with brass buttons, a light blue silk blouse, and polished pumps. The outfit made her butt poke out more than normal, and she had her hair pulled up into a fashionable ponytail that brought out her true features.

I wouldn't know if she had gotten dressed up for me or if that was her normal routine, but either way, the woman was beautiful, and I wanted her. I guess she must have felt my presence because she looked up and saw me staring at her. Though our glances were short, she knew what was on my mind, and I clearly expressed that without saying a word.

She went back to dealing with her staff, and I made my way downstairs to start my move into my station. I figured if Michelle wanted her stuff moved too, she would let me know. Two hours passed before she made her way over to my area, and I knew once she noticed a picture of Samantha was missing, she would come looking for it.

"You sure about this?" she asked me with a look on her face that informed me she was only talking about us and everything that came with the both of us.

"You waiting on me to run a front-page editorial on what's in my heart?" I replied. She made a move to pick up the picture of Samantha.

"Leave her there!" I snapped at her. "Are you coming over here with us or are you staying over there on your own?" I asked her as we stared into each other's eyes. "And I'm not talking about your cubicle either!"

She stared back at me with tears building up in her eyes. I pulled two sheets of Kleenex out of its dispenser and gave them to her. She never made a move to wipe her tears as they flowed freely down her face.

"Yes," she stated as we continued to stare into each other's eyes.

"How am I supposed to know that that's what you truly want and need, Michelle?" She slowly walked over toward me and kissed me on the cheek as I asked her to the day before.

"Are you satisfied with that?" she asked. I grabbed her hand and led her to her private corner in the *Herald* and kissed her until she got enough.

"Now, I'm satisfied, Mrs. Allen, but the question is, are you?"

"Are you talking about the Mrs. Allen part, Mr. Allen?" she asked.

"Yes!" I replied.

"Then yes, I am satisfied with that!" she stated.

"How am I supposed to know that, Michelle?"

"For starters," she said, kissing me until I had enough, "you did mention until death do us part, didn't you, Mr. Allen?"

"That's exactly what I said, Mrs. Allen."

"Then I guess this conversation is over, isn't it?"

"I wanted it over with yesterday, woman," I said as I gently kissed her forehead.

Peterson's whistle caught both our attention. "You two, right now!" he said in a demanding tone while pointing toward his office.

"Damn, is he upset?" I asked Michelle.

"There's only one way to find out, so bring your scared ass on," she said. Michelle straightened up the collar on her blouse and her jacket.

"Ladies first," I stated as we shuffled into Pete's office.

"Close the door, and draw my blinds," he barked out as he looked at us both. Once we did as he requested, he ordered us to sit down. He gave her the meanest stare he could come up with. "Allen, what did she say?" he asked, continuing to stare the meanest at Michelle.

"She said yes, Pete."

Pete broke down his mean streak and started smiling as he sat back in his chair with his arms folded across his chest.

"Congratulations, Ms. Evans, or should I say, Mrs. Allen?" Pete said with a smile. Michelle looked over at me and slapped my shoulder. "You've discussed this?"

"Girl, the man acts like your father and gave me more flack behind you than Mona did," I said as I rubbed my shoulder.

"Mona! Oh no you didn't, Trey Allen," she said as she stood up.

"Girl, stop your drama, and meet us for lunch," Judge Evans said through the conference speaker on Pete's desk.

"Aunt Gwen?" Michelle asked, her voice full of shock.

"Yeah, girl, because we have a wedding to plan," Dr. Sanchez said over the conference speaker as she and Judge Evans laughed.

"I am so through with the both of you heifers," Michelle said to Dr. Sanchez and Judge Evans before killing the call by hanging up on them. She turned and looked at me with a silly schoolgirl look on her face.

"I didn't know all of this was going to happen, girl, so get on his ass," I said as I pointed toward Pete.

"Ohh, you'll get over it, young lady, and anything shorter than the best man, I'm bringing the both of your asses up on inappropriate conduct charges on the job site, which gives me the discretion to fire the both of you. Do I make myself clear?"

I couldn't filter out if he was playing or serious, but he deserved the spot. I told Pete he had it, then got up and shook his hand.

"Now, the both of you sit down," he insisted. I'm like a gatekeeper around this place and a damn good one too! You, young lady, have raised the concerns of a few leaders in this city to the point that my phone is ringing about a possible dinner table conversation. I want to know what it is that you two are working on, minus the bullshit."

"The police department closed out on more than four cases that were ruled suicides but were actual murders, and all of them were African-American females, Mr. Peterson," Michelle explained.

"Damn! You two know this for sure?" he asked.

"For sure," Michelle replied.

"Are you giving us up, Pete?" I asked him, and even though I questioned him at that very moment, he knew his reputation as editor was going to be put on the line.

"How dare you ask me a question like that, Allen!" He went in his drawer and retrieved a cigar and a lighter. I knew I cut him real deep with that question because he kept his eyes on me as he lit his cigar. "I haven't lit one of these in over five years, and I've waited on a day that I could face the city from this mountaintop as the damn chief of this newspaper.

"You think the mayor, city council, city manager, the sheriff, city attorney's office, NAACP, and any other activist will be on my ass?" he asked as he puffed on his cigar.

"They'll be after your head, Pete!" I replied softly.

"That's the way I prefer it, Allen, and whatever you two do, don't let up until you're satisfied. Do I make myself clear?"

"You got it, Pete."

"Now, Mrs. Allen-to-be, you're officially off the clock for a few days, and the only time I want to see your face around this place is when I pass up that employee group picture downstairs. I don't want the judge calling my office every hour, wanting to talk to you, so give her your time, and that way Mona won't complain either."

"Hold up!" I said with my attention now turned toward Pete. "Why is it that when you refer to Gwendolyn Evans, you call her 'Judge,' but when it comes down to Dr. Mona Sanchez, it's always 'Mona'?"

"Allen!"

"Oh, hell no! To hell with the supervisor shit. This is man-to-man. Baby, I hate for you to hear this, but it's either him or me," I said as I kissed her lips.

Michelle was confused as to where I was about to go, but Pete just let me know that he was banging the doctor.

"Pete, I'm asking you one time as respectful as I can without compromising your position. You and Mona or do I have to go to work as a journalist on you?"

"Damn it, Allen," he said as he sat up and put his cigar out.

"Oh, you and Mona, Mr. Peterson?" Michelle asked as she placed her hands over her mouth surprisingly.

"Damn it, you two. I didn't say a word, and please don't say anything about it," he begged in a way.

"I can't believe you, boss."

"Mrs. Allen, I am a man, am I not?"

"I'm sorry, boss, but I have to at least work Mona until she gives you up. Hell, you've been the mystery man between me and my aunt Gwen for almost two and a half years now."

Pete looked over at me for some help, but I wasn't throwing out a lifeline for his creeping ass.

"I'm not getting in the way, Pete, and don't blame me for listening. Hell, that's why you pay me," I said as I laughed.

"Okay, the both of you get your nosy asses out of my office, and if she gets on my ass about this, you'll be receiving a shitty gift from me. Get out!" he shouted and slammed the door behind us.

Michelle and I walked back down to her cubicle, and I made her sit down on my lap. We sat there in silence for a few minutes. "My life is about to change again, and I can't believe I've let you come in less than a week and turn my world a flip," Michelle said.

"You don't have control over what God orders, woman, so stop trippin'!"

"Trey, I don't even know what you like to eat or anything."

"You know that I want you with me, right?"

"Yeah, but—" I stopped her.

"Girl, do you hear me trippin' about not knowing what you like and what you don't like?"

"No!" she replied.

"Then that ought to be special to you."

"More like insane, boy!"

"Insane?"

"Yes, insane!" she said with a smile on her face as she caressed my face with two of her fingers. "You're either the craziest man on the planet for wanting to marry me after knowing me less than a week or a fool for love."

"I'll be guilty of them both, and people will have a lot to talk about too. You know they'll be placing bets on how long we'll last, right?"

"Do you care about that, Trey?"

"I was a winner the moment you kissed my cheek."

"You thought I forgot, didn't you?" she asked.

"I didn't have any plans on letting you forget, Michelle."

"So where do we go from here?" she asked.

"Simple, Michelle, it's me, you, Samantha, and Darius, and I'm selling my parents' house. You plan the wedding and find a house that you love, and I'll be happy about it all. Before I say 'I do,' can you cook?"

"I can't boil water, Trey."

"I guess we'll be eating out of cans and restaurants then."

"Boy, I can cook! Look at these hips," she said, standing to raise her suit jacket to show me her ass.

"You might want to put a halt on doing that again because I'm fighting to let you hang on to your little goodies until our wedding night. So please lower the jacket, ma'am," I said sarcastically.

She started unbuttoning it, took the jacket off, pulled her skirt up on her fine hips, grabbed her purse, and left the building, shaking her ass in a monster stride.

TRAPPED

We all finally got a week of full rest from Darius's waking up, fighting, and running from his demon. Outside of the *Herald*, it was Darius and me. If I intended to catch his clues about what was destroying him from the inside out, I had to keep trusting in Mona's thirty years of experience dealing with children. Though Michelle dropped tips at times about my having some level of say so on our wedding plans, I just couldn't pull myself away from Darius long enough to think about anything else. It was clear that Darius and I were the lone riders in a personal crusade, and I had to show him that it was me and him. I also had to teach him how to be stiff when it came down to his dreams.

He was to the point that he didn't cry anymore, but asking him not to be scared or pushing his little shivering body away was out of the question. To think of pushing him away as he whispered, "Bad, Uncle Trey, bad!" Well, that would be cruel!

Today was going to be our third date together, Michelle, Darius, and me. I didn't want to come to grips with the reality of my using Darius, but besides my sticking close to the little fellow in case he revealed something, I was also trying to stay out of Michelle's bed until our wedding. Though three weeks was a good limit for me to have had to wait for sex, this was my choice, and she really appreciated it.

Five of the largest churches in North Waco held an annual picnic down at the city's park. Since the park was about a ten-mile stretch with its elevated hillsides, one could view parts of the city from on high with awe. Waco residents were proud of the park, with its vast picnic areas, its secluded neighborhood living, the trails, and the city zoo, not to mention the beautiful Brazos River that lazily flowed at its edge.

I've always appreciated the many people, whether they were white, black, Hispanic, Asian, or Middle Eastern, coming together to show their support for a unified neighborhood. All that brought about enough food to feed the entire city, and with a lot of neighborhood restaurants joining in to provide free food, it was an all-day buffet!

All the church choirs took center stage at different times during the day to provide the masses with food for the soul. Though neither choir ever actually challenged the other, it was a known fact that there was a deep-rooted competition going on among a few of the choirs. This undercover competition was so huge that people came in from as far away as Chicago and Los Angeles to witness the "battle of the choirs," but all in a good way.

I felt as if I were at work all day because Pete had at least 20 percent of the *Herald* on this event—from the construction of the stages to the final prayer at the event's closing. One thing Donald was good at, and I didn't have a problem giving the brother his props, was that of being a prolific speaker, and as a minister, his words had the fish at the banks of the river, stealing his anointed words from God. Darius held a seat on my shoulders while my wife-to-be stood at my side, shouting her continuous "amens" and "hallelujahs" each time the Word touched her spirit.

Whether or not Darius knew what Donald was saying or not, when the masses clapped, he clapped! What really caught me by surprise was when the three of us were leaving the park, we ran into Donald. Darius was reluctant to greet him. There wasn't a Sunday that went by that Darius didn't run to hug Donald, but this time, he wasn't as quick to make contact.

"My favorite little person in the world," Donald said as he greeted Darius. He knelt down to get his normal hug from Darius.

This time, however, it was weird. Darius latched on to Michelle's left leg with both arms and stared a hollow glare back at Donald.

"Darius, that's so rude," Michelle said, looking down at him.

Standing back with a fake smile on his face, Donald quickly made an excuse for him, saying Darius was probably worn out from all the fun he enjoyed all day.

"Well, I hope you all enjoyed yourselves. God knows I did! By the way, I appreciate you all sending me an invitation to your wedding. Everybody is talking about this wedding, and the fact that your family belongs to our big church, we were hoping you would change your minds and have the wedding there instead of the convention center."

The truth of the matter was he really didn't care about the family or members of the church. He wanted the spotlight on the church, his church.

"Not that we haven't considered it, Donald, but this is what Michelle wants, and I'm rollin' with it. I think the family will appreciate the space nonetheless." I reached down and picked up Darius.

"Bad, Uncle Trey," he whispered once I held him up in my arms. The two of us looked eye to eye for a few seconds. Then I heard Michelle's reminder that Samantha told her in her dream, "Trust him."

"Listen, Donald, it's been a long day, and I don't mean to be rude, but I need to get my crew back on our own grounds." I shook the brother's hand and didn't give him time, room, or opportunity to say another word. I just grabbed Michelle's hand and made a straight quest to the car.

As we walked to the car, Michelle whispered, "Talk to me." She sensed something wasn't right.

When I explained that Darius had said Donald was bad, she was confused and said, "What?"

"Michelle, get in the car, baby, and we'll discuss this on the way home."

I fastened Darius in his car seat and quickly walked to the driver's side to get in. I glanced back to see if Donald was still getting his dose of praises from his groupies, but I couldn't see him through the crowd. I was a few miles away from the park before I said a word, and with the glances Michelle was giving me, I knew she was tired of waiting.

Before she could say a word, I quickly told her that I didn't want to influence Darius into saying something he thinks we want him to say. Whatever it is that he's trying to tell us, I wanted him to say it on his own accord.

"Say what, baby?" Michelle asked.

"As I picked him up, he whispered that Donald is b-a-d," I told her, spelling the word because I knew Darius was listening attentively.

Michelle slowly turned to look back at him and smiled as she pinched his little nose. "So how do you feel about this, Trey?" she asked as she continued to play with Darius.

"I want him to say it again. One thing he was totally aware of was whispering it to me and not letting Donald hear what he said."

"So what if he doesn't say it right off, Trey?"

"Michelle, as soon as Darius saw him, he held on to your leg. He was scared."

"Trey, you just can't base anything on that. He was just hugging the man around his neck not long ago at church, if you recall," she justifiably mentioned.

"You're the one who advised me to trust him, Michelle!" I said, frustrated. She quickly responded that she still wants me to trust him but that I couldn't just go building a case on the man until there were facts. She continued that she was aware that I had some deep-rooted issues with Donald, and if I had my way, I would race to pin Hope's death on him.

"You plan to give him fair warning that you're lookin' at him now or keepin' your head until this evolves again?"

"Damn it!" I was so frustrated that I struck the steering wheel.

"Trey, please. You're scaring Darius!" Michelle cried out.

I did a straight shot to Hope's gravesite for one of my private thinking sessions. It was the first time Michelle had ever visited her grave but a frequent one for Darius and me.

I jumped out of the car and did a beeline straight to Hope's grave. When I got there, I saw evidence that the brother I wanted to kill for possibly killing my sister had visited her grave and placed flowers on it.

"From Reverend D. Simms, I miss you, Hope," the card said. Something inside of me dictated my next move. I wadded up the card, picked the flowers up, and walked over to the nearest trash bin. I hated that Michelle was witnessing my acts of anger, but if she vowed to marry me with all my kinks, this was one she had to accept. I saw Darius trying to drag Michelle toward Hope's grave by her index finger as fast as she would allow him to. I stood motionless and watched her kneel down to embrace Darius as a mother would.

As soon as I saw her reach up to wipe her face, I knew she was crying for Darius's loss and hers too. I walked up on them in time to hear Darius say, "Mama take it." I had heard him say those words quite a few times in the past two weeks or so.

"What did she take, Darius?" Michelle asked him with some concern. He ran to me crying when I walked up. "Trey, Mama take it!"

"Darius, if you can't tell me more than that, what am I supposed to do, nephew?" Michelle could hear the aggravation in my voice.

"Trey, you stop that!" Michelle snapped, taking Darius from my arms.

"Come here, baby." He wrapped his arms around her neck. "Stop crying, Darius, and tell me what Mama took that has you so upset?"

He just said it again, looking at me, wanting so badly for me to understand. "Darius, where did mama take it?" Michelle asked him. He looked at her for a second to register what she had just asked. He started wiggling out of her arms. Once she finally put him down, he gave us his last and final plea for us to listen!

"Mama, take it, Trey," he said as he slapped at her grave. "Darius, you stop that!" I said.

Michelle interrupted me with a stronger tone. "Look at him, Trey! He's trying to get something across to us." She asked him again where did his Mama take it. He pointed straight at the ground, down to her grave site.

"Mama, take it, Uncle Trey." He hugged my leg and started crying. I looked at Michelle, suddenly realizing what he was crying for and what he was trying so desperately to tell us. But how could it be? It didn't make sense!

"What is it, Trey?" Michelle asked.

I told her to wait while I went to the car to get the photograph of Darius sleeping. As soon as I returned with it, I looked down at Hope's grave with a search for reasoning. "The first time he ever said 'Mama take it' was when he saw this," I explained, showing her and pointing to the picture.

"What?"

"Look, Michelle. Darius's blanket always covered him when he slept."

Michelle looked again at the picture and back up at me. She handed Darius the picture, and he immediately pointed to the blanket in the picture and bent down. "Mama take it, Uncle Trey!" He again pointed toward her grave, still repeating those words.

"Okay, little man, Uncle Trey understands now." As I lifted him up off the ground, I reassured him that I truly understood what he had been trying to tell me all along.

"I was there at the funeral, Michelle, and no I didn't see it, so don't start!"

"Maybe he did, Trey."

"Come on, Michelle, she had on a cream-colored gown. There's no way I could have missed that with all the colors in the damn blanket!" I insisted.

"Darius, look at Aunt Michelle." He reached out for her, and she took him from my arms. "You tell your Uncle Trey where mama took your blanket, baby." He didn't hesitate to respond once her question registered in his little mind. "Mama take it, Trey!" Once again, he pointed down to her grave.

"Get in the car!" I told her. I walked away from Hope's grave, staring at the photograph. "Where does Mona live?" I asked as Michelle began giving me her address.

"I'm calling Dunbar to have him meet us there, and maybe they can help make sense of this and deal with Donald being 'bad' in Darius's eyes. This may be the break I've been looking for, but even if it's not, we need to give it a look for Darius's sake."

Michelle leaned over to kiss me on my cheek. "Trust him, Trey," she said in a whisper-like tone so she wouldn't disturb Darius who was beginning to fall asleep. I was fortunate to find Dunbar at the station as we made our way back into North Waco. It was another thirty minutes before we all made it to Mona's, and as I entered her living room, the first thing I found outside of all the beautiful things inside her home was Pete's favorite cologne drifting in and out of my nostrils. If he hadn't just left, then he was still somewhere in the house.

After explaining our encounters during the past two hours, Mona and Dunbar were divided. "Let's get one thing clear, Allen. I'm not about to go arrest Simms on the grounds that your nephew says that he is a bad man. Hell, I've arrested six bad men today because they broke a law that they were guilty of and not because a group of kids said they were bad!" He wasn't finished.

"Second of all, I'm not going to bring him in for questioning or visit his home. If I want to ask the man anything, I can do that when he calls, breathing down my neck about neglecting or not doing enough to solve this case. Just so you know, the man has every official he could find to ride down on the chief concerning your sister's death. I can't see why a guilty man would push so damn hard for results!"

"Well, as I see it, that's his way of keeping tabs on you, Mr. Dunbar," Mona stated.

"Are you implying that the man is guilty, ma'am?"

"No, I'm not, but I am addressing the behavior of a criminal mind-set. The more he pushes his influences past the thresholds of the chief's desk, the mayor's office, the city manager's desk, and city council members, it gives him an overview of where you are at all times and lets him know how close you are to solving this case." Mona said, making it clear.

"I don't think the chief would leak any information in your investigation, Mr. Dunbar, but the previously mentioned officials are being told something to hold them at bay, and I would gather that your boss hasn't given you a moment's rest either." Dunbar sat there staring back at Mona as if she was on target about everything she had just said.

"I'm not moving on the man based on the grounds of a kid saying that he's bad, and that's the end of that, people! If something arises that warrants my attention to arrest the man, I won't hesitate to do so. Until then, I'm giving you all sound advice. If you go off half-cocked and give the man fair warning that you're looking at him in the slightest way, guilty or not, he'll arm himself with some more ways to wiggle out of this. So stay clear, and let me do my job! You people have a nice day." With that, he left Mona's home.

"He's right about the man finding more ways to stay elusive. If you're going to trust in Darius, Trey, you can't change up your pattern of how you deal with Mr. Simms because he'll detect it as soon as he comes across you. You don't know for a fact that it was him, and if the police department didn't find a reason to at least make him a possible suspect, then don't ruin any possibility that you might be right."

I asked Mona what her take was on the blanket issue. She responded, "If you're asking me for some advice, I'm going to tell you to raise Hope back up out of the ground and open the casket!"

"Come on, Doc. I was there standing over the casket myself, for God's sake!"

"Then why are we discussing this, Trey? Is it because there could be a possibility or because of the compassion you have for that child in there?"

"Please, Mona, spare me with the physiological bull! We are not in your office, and I'm sure as hell not your client!"

"This isn't about me. It's about you and what your conscious is telling you to do. So we either end this conversation or get with Gwendolyn on this, so she can get together with the right judge that will grant the order to exhume the body. Whatever problem we may face, we have to be prepared because one thing is for sure, and you should seriously take into account, if in fact the blanket is in there, it was placed in there for a specific reason."

I looked over at Michelle, and she pointed at her heart and then at me indicating that I should trust what I was feeling.

"I'm tired of funerals, and now we're sitting here talking about repeating the process. No disrespect to you in your own house, Mona, but this is crazy!" I turned to reach for my keys, trying to sort through everything. "Michelle, you got Darius?"

"What kind of question is that, Trey? Just go do whatever it is you are going to do, and either I'll be here or at my place." I kissed her and grabbed the photo and left. Despite what Dunbar or Mona advised me not to do, I had to go ask Donald about this blanket.

The fact that I stood over Hope's casket long enough to have noticed all those damn colors in the blanket but not see it did not make sense, and even the notion of questioning myself sounded crazy. Nevertheless, it was either ask Donald or raise Hope for Darius, and I wasn't feeling the latter!

It took me about ten minutes to get to his house and another ten minutes to make up my mind about listening to Dunbar and Mona or just asking the dude! By the time I made up my mind to stop doubting and ask, he was pulling out of his driveway. I didn't question whether I should follow Donald or not, I just did! I followed him to a convenience store. Once there, I intended to pull up as if I needed to get gas. Instead, I parked where he couldn't see me, but I had a clear view of him. Seeing him place a carton of Kool cigarettes on the counter interested me because I thought he didn't smoke anymore. Maybe, I thought to myself, he was about to visit someone who smoked.

One thing I did know about a street hustler is that his habits never change. Donald exited the store looking left to right as if he had a reason to scan the area for good or bad. Wherever he was going and whoever he was going to see, he was being extra cautious because he was adjusting his mirrors. I knew right then that the person he was going to see was not part of his flock.

It was five minutes after we left the store that I came to the conclusion that he was going in and out of directions that didn't make sense, so I knew he was trying to make sure he was not being followed. He drove from North Waco to the south side and took the loop just to come back to the north side again then ended up driving into the parking lot of the new mall in Waco.

One thing I had going for myself was plenty of cover! The mall sat in the center of a huge parking lot, and with all the people coming and going, there was no way he could have spotted me. After about ten minutes of his sitting in his car, it was evident that he was waiting on someone. As the sun began to set, I got out of my car and walked into Dillard's with a crowd of people near and watched him from inside the glass doors. He kept looking in all directions for whoever was supposed to show up. Finally I spotted a woman who kept looking suspiciously up and down the rows of parked cars. She was one of his girls, and like Kat, once Donald left the "pimping scene," she went down in her already low life.

Just a few more feet, little mama. She was approaching Donald's car. Once she spotted him, she got in the passenger's side. Their conversation lasted just a few minutes, and she wasn't out of the car a hot second when I heard his car start up. As she passed under one of the light poles, I saw the carton of cigarettes. I wondered what could she have traded for them?

I wasn't interested in Donald from this point on because there was this gutter girl down on her luck, and though I couldn't see her having a personal motive to kill Hope, I still wanted to find out where she was holding up at. It would have been foolish of me to follow her on foot because she might have had a trick waiting on her in a car somewhere nearby. So I had to sprint back to my car and hope like hell I didn't lose her.

I was right about her trick laying low and waiting on her in the nearby apartments that overlooked the mall. Though I couldn't get a clear look at the dude driving the car, I knew they were headed straight back to the gutter grounds. I hadn't been back home long enough to know where the dope traps were or who was pumping the dope, but I knew the smell of a dope dealer when I was near one. The trick pulled over at the corner between two well-known streets and ran up to a parked car. It had at least ten grand worth of accessories on it. Obviously, this was her dope man. She was in and out and back in the car with her trick. Donald was still having compassion for the girls and was helping them out all this time.

After stopping again, this time for beer, the two of them made their way to the motel on the far edges of East Waco. It wasn't until the guy got out of the car that I saw his true identity. He was a middle-aged white guy that limped and walked with a cane. He most likely waited on a monthly government check of some sort because of his disability.

I gave them about twenty minutes before I left the area to get Dunbar on the line. Twenty minutes was long enough to have pushed what mattered most in their veins.

I pulled up at the McDonald's near the Interstate and called Dunbar from there. "Waco Police Department, how can I help you?" came from the familiar voice of the desk sergeant.

"Officer Dunbar, please. This is Trey Allen." As usual I was told to hold.

"What's up, guy?"

"So you just sitting there hoping somebody calls you?"

"Up yours, Allen, and get off the bull! What do you want?"

"I need you to crash a party for me, just to see if our object is in the hands of one of Donald's old workhorses."

"What are you up to, Allen?"

"Look, meet me at the McDonald's on East Interstate 35, and I'll explain it all to you when you get here."

"Six minutes, and this better be good, Allen!"

"Oh, like you were on top of some major shit!" He hung up the phone, and I went inside the McDonald's to have some fries and wait.

By the time he arrived and I explained the past two hours to him, he talked his smack to me for almost putting the investigation in jeopardy, but he had to follow up on my request. "So how do you plan to get in the room?" I asked.

"I'll wait until they come out and ask for the key, or would you prefer that I kick the damn door down?"

I didn't give a damn; I just wanted him to get in! It was an hour before the girl and the old dude came out, and Dunbar waited on them to reach the car before he confronted them. Whatever he told them, both of them were out of the car and sitting on the front hood as he searched the entire car down. He sent the old man on his way once he finished and walked the girl back up to the room, closing the door. He was in there for about fifteen minutes before the door opened, and he walked out.

"You can count your lucky stars tonight," he stated as he got into my car.

"So what's up?"

"Your sister was the Feds' link to putting Donald away for ten calendar years, and she wouldn't do it. From what the girl says, Donald started allowing them to get high and supplied them all the drugs they needed. Your sister wanted Donald off the streets in exchange for her silence. Well, Kat was pissed because it was her time to be this so-called bottom whore, but she never had her chance."

"That's some bull! I know for a fact that Kat was in charge of overseeing the rest of the girls once Hope left Donald."

"Hold your horses, Allen, and get a hold of your hat because Kat offered twenty grand for the death of your sister. The girl said that Kat had gotten in real good with Hope, but when the time came for the hit on your sister to go down, no one wanted the money because they knew Donald would find out about it, and he would end up with all of it anyway. Long story short, Kat ended up telling Donald that she had the money in a plea to keep him, but he started using it to pump dope into Kat and the rest of them."

"So who ended up in the house, Dunbar?"

"She said the only one out of all the girls that wanted Hope out of the picture was Kat!"

"So how am I lucky?" I didn't understand.

"She never stated that Donald knew about the plot to kill Hope, but what whore would do all that to get closer to her pimp so she could rule the rest of the girls? She's too far gone to be helpful because if taken off the streets, she'll say anything to get back on them for a shot. I let her to keep her dope and the money that Donald gave her, but I told her that if I even think that she told Donald that I had asked about him, I would see to it that she goes without her dope for weeks!"

"So we start looking at a conspiracy to commit murder but we still don't have enough to do that 'cause we are depending on what some half-dead woman had to say? Forget it!"

We had to keep grinding for an opening until something else broke. It was after 11:00 p.m. when I made it to Michelle's place, and as odd as that was, I was sticking my own key in the door at her place. She and Darius had bathed and were asleep in the bed together. I knelt down on the floor to get face-to-face with Michelle and kissed her lips. Her eyes came open slowly, and she smiled at me. "You are a very beautiful woman when you sleep!"

She touched my face and asked how things went.

"You let me worry about this end, and you just make sure our wedding is perfect."

She took a whiff and said, "You could have at least brought me some French fries too, Trey!"

I placed my hand in front of my face and let out a puff of air to smell my own breath. I couldn't detect one fry. "What are you talking about, woman?" I asked innocently.

"I'll shower and catch the spare room because this bed ain't big enough for the two Allen men," I whispered as I kissed her and left to shower.

The more I thought about Hope, the more I couldn't help seeing how much she really cared about Donald. I guess once she understood that the Feds wanted him bad enough that they were pulling out every avenue they could, she figured getting pregnant was her way of having a piece of him in case they did get him. I understood why she never admitted that Darius was his. She knew that coming to church was a play, but she hung in there to see if God was going to eventually pull him through. I guess she never had plans to really follow through on her word to Mama after all.

Hearing about the plot to kill Hope was an eye-opener for me, and I also realized how much Kat loved Donald too. I was willing to bet that Kat was the person who gave those girls on Michelle's lists their lethal injections. She'd been fighting for the number one spot since she met him. Her telling me that she was already dead was an indication that she lost everything when she lost Spoon. Perhaps she lived by the old saying, "If I can't have you, nobody else will," but she should have taken Donald with her and not Hope!

I tossed and turned for at least two hours that night. My mind took me back to the day Kat and I had our encounter. She knew Donald was on his way out and tried to offer herself and the rest of the girls to me. For her, to have offered me five grand for a session meant that the other girls changed their minds about not doing Hope that week or that day.

I guess sleep finally caught up with me and so did Darius and Michelle. Feeling and smelling a mixture of vanilla and lavender on her skin as she lay next to me was a level of bliss for me. Whatever time of the night it was when they came to join me was a sure indication that she didn't want to be without me. It was after ten in the morning, and if I hadn't forced myself to get out of bed, I'm sure we would have still been asleep way past twelve. I went ahead and started breakfast to give Darius and Michelle time to sleep until I was halfway done.

There was something about the smell of bacon cooking that aroused or summoned people from the depths of their sleep. Darius showed up, trotting in the kitchen with a freshly lotioned face, and that was enough to know that Michelle was doing her thing and needed her privacy. Not having a man to wake up to for almost four years meant having herself together before I could have some attention.

We had another full day to spend together, and though we weren't in a rush to get to the mall as we had planned, relaxing was our main objective. I couldn't stall a minute more on the thought of all three of us eating at the same time because Darius, the dictator, wasn't trying to hear or feel none of that!

Michelle finally exited the bathroom, and though I hadn't seen her yet, the perfume she was wearing was just for me, and no one could tell me anything else. When she did finally show up, I had one word to say to her, "Radiant!"

"Thank you, Mr. Allen," she said with a smile and a kiss.

"I guess I've broken one of my mother's rules this morning, but I'm blaming it all on you," I said to her to make her feel some guilt.

"And what would that be, if you don't mind me asking?" she asked, resting her hands on her hips.

"No sweets before breakfast," I replied as I wiped the corners of my mouth with my napkin. She couldn't help but laugh her schoolgirl laugh.

It was good seeing Michelle smile. I cracked open quite a few photo albums that she had around the house, and I also caught a glimpse of her motherly side. There was no doubt that she was honoring the opportunity to raise Darius as a mother who never got an opportunity to raise her only child. The fact that he would never have his birth mother and she would never have her only child made them bond in a respectable and wonderful way. Darius loved the motherly attention, and the fact that he showed his affection for Michelle made our situation even better.

As we approached the mall, she knelt down to make sure Darius was straight, kissed his forehead, and stood back up. Then she tilted her head back, and we made our way into the center of what seemed like two thousand people.

I went into one store and bought something; Michelle went into three stores and bought nothing. She wasn't feelin' anything, she explained, but after my four stores and four purchases and Michelle's continued routine of not finding anything in twelve stores, I finally put the brakes on everything really quickly!

"Baby, I'm not going into another store to see nine things, ask eleven questions, try on six outfits, and walk out with you empty-handed! Do you love me?"

She stood there, feeling guilty for the torture she was putting me through. "Yes, I love you!"

"Then if you expect me to be able to keep up with you whenever we go shopping, you will have to feed your man, girl, between all these stops! I can't do all this on a quarter tank of gas!" She started smiling and took me by the hand.

"So what's the game plan, little mama?"

"There's a Luby's Cafeteria on the other end of the mall. In case you can't tell, it's been a long time since I've shopped, and things have changed so much that it has taken me out of my comfort zone."

"Listen, woman, from this point on, can I tell you what I love on you and that way you can get something for me and for you?"

"Well, why haven't you said anything before now, Trey?"

"Every time I said, 'Baby that's nice,' you said, 'It doesn't fit right,' and you put it back."

"Do you want to go back and get the ones that you liked?" she asked.

"Well, I'm glad you asked and here's a list of the stores I want to go back to," I replied.

"No, you didn't, Trey!"

"Girl, you better take this list," I said as I grabbed her hand and placed the list in the palm of her hand. Like most women, Michelle wanted to know what I was going to eat, and I've learned to remain quiet. Number one rule, ladies go first and get to the cashier, that way you can avoid her shopping for food like she shops for clothes.

"Oh that looks good," Michelle said as she admired my grilled fish. "Would you like to taste some?" I asked as she grinned a yes.

"Nope," I said, putting my next bite into my mouth!

"You are so wrong for doing that, Mr. Allen," she said, frowning.

I looked at her and smiled as I pushed my plate in front of her and took the remainder of her roast beef. I knew once she didn't complain about the switch, I wouldn't be getting my fish back, and it was cool!

It seemed like Michelle and I were on a date even though Darius was with us. He stayed in his own little world, enjoying his own food and humming because it was good. We stuffed ourselves and couldn't finish dessert, and as soon as I heard "Oh Lord" from Michelle, I knew shopping was over!

"Baby, can we shop another day?" she asked. Looking at my watch, I saw that we had five hours before our movie started. "Okay, but what will we do next?"

"I'm telling you right now, I'm going to see that movie, so if you want to sleep, and you will, it will be me and Darius!"

"Trey, I'm going," she said with a sly smirk on her face.

"Yeah, right, Michelle," I replied.

And to show her how serious I was about making it to that movie, I went and bought the tickets.

Out of all the people in the mall, I spotted Donald. I didn't say anything to Michelle, and since he was walking up the other side, I just continued on as if I didn't see him. Unfortunately, though, he wasn't having it. He cut a path straight to us.

"Baby, do you see who I see?" Michelle asked.

"Unfortunately, and I was hoping to just walk past him."

"Avoid the reverend? Now, Trey," she said in a joking manner, "how could you?"

"I'm glad to see the two of you, and you too, my little man," Donald said, rubbing Darius on his head with his left hand and raising his right hand to shake mine.

Suddenly, I felt like hell opened its gate. Surely, God knew I was shaking hands with Satan himself, and Darius . . . he was fully aware of what I was feeling because I felt him moving behind me, hiding from the very thing that haunted him since the death of his mother. At that moment, I knew that the bastard killed my sister, and he left his own child in the house to fend for himself as Hope lay lifeless in a pool of blood.

I took a good firm grip on his hand, bringing a twitch to his face. All I could see was crushing his ass, just like he had done to my sister and to Darius and to me! I heard an inner voice shout, "Let him go!" I

RAISING HOPE FOR DARIUS

obeyed, but not before I rolled his wrist to expose a clear look at this gold-beaded lion's head ring with rubies in its eyes.

"So why are you so glad to see us, Rev?" I asked, releasing his hand.

"I don't like guessing when it comes to getting a gift out for someone, so please do me the favor, and just tell me what you want, and save me the legwork."

"Cash would be fine, Reverend Simms," Michelle said.

He asked if we were sure, and Michelle told him we planned to start a savings for Darius's college fund.

"Then cash it is! Well, I hope to see you all in church tomorrow," he said as he walked off.

Michelle was so nervous that she trembled. I saw three young ladies about to approach us and gave them the rest of our afternoon by handing them the tickets I had insisted we purchase. They were in complete shock as I told them to have a nice afternoon and to enjoy the movie. We left the mall and rode home in total silence.

Michelle knew I had some heavy thoughts on my mind. "Baby, what are we going to do now?"

"I'm calling Dunbar before I change my mind and shoot the bastard myself."

She tried to redirect my thinking. "If you do, then there won't be any us, and you will be failing Darius, Trey."

Those were the last words she spoke on our way back to her place.

Rat Trap

The doorbell rang, and I knew it couldn't be anyone other than Dunbar. After the phone conversation we had, he had mixed feelings about my encounter, but my having more than a gut feeling was placing Donald "Spoon" Simms at risk. Dunbar knew I was on the borderline of doing something to him. As I opened the door, I saw a neatly groomed white boy standing beside Dunbar. This guy looked as if he had just fallen off the cover of the golf digest.

"Trey, I apologize for not giving you a heads-up on me bringing company, but on the way over, I thought it was appropriate for this situation," Dunbar explained.

"Please come in." My voice was hollow.

"Trey, this is Sam Watkins, assistant DA, and I think it's important that you hear him out on this before things get too far out of hand."

"So what's up, Detective? Are you building a case against me on pre-prosecution?" I said in a cold tone and by the look on Dunbar's face, it sunk deep. He knew how I was going to take him bringing a prosecutor between or in on everything that we'd done, but more so, I knew he was really doing it to keep me off Donald!

"Trey, come on, man, lighten up, dude! Yeah, I can understand how this looks, but I'm on your side, and I'm doing everything I can to make sure that if Donald Simms is, in fact, responsible for Hope's murder—"

I jumped up. "What the hell do you mean 'if' he's responsible, Dunbar? You and I both know this, don't we?" We stared into each other's eyes, but he never responded. "Yeah, I know you feel it, Detective! It's that exact feeling that keeps you from sleeping at night, huh?" I asked with a smooth hood-like swagger.

"Are you going to listen to what Sam has to say or not?" I could hear the irritation in his voice. We both knew he was playing the good professional police officer in front of Sam, and that pissed me off!

"I'm listening, Sam," I said but continued to stare at Dunbar.

"Mr. Allen, according to—"

"Drop the formalities, Sam. We're out of the office, if you don't mind!"

Sam looked over at Dunbar before starting again.

"According to what evidence we do have, I truly believe that he killed your sister. In fact, I am the one who advised him to do a second search of your parents' home and Donald's place for two reasons, one being that he showed up at the courthouse trying to get custody of your nephew, and two, it took him too long to inquire about the little boy. If I thought that Darius was my son, I wouldn't have allowed him to fall into the hand of CPS."

"So why are you here, Sam?" I asked curiously.

"One, to keep you from killing the man, and two, to ask you to give us just a little more time to push this guy into a corner. I can't talk about what my office is doing to get this guy, but I can tell you this. If we can't find the key evidence we need to convict him for your sister's murder, I want him locked away for having knowledge about the deaths of the prostitutes who worked for him."

This comment had me turning back to Dunbar for answers. "He talking about the girls on our list?"

"Same ones, Trey!"

"So, Sam, you doing all this to help cover your boss's ass and the chief of police's ass too, or are you trying to raise your status in the ranks?"

"All bull aside, Allen, my boss is an arrogant bastard, and I think the furniture needs to be changed around, if you get my drift?"

I had to ask him if he was using this case as an example.

"That would be something my boss would do, Allen. I'm only interested in catching a murderer and cleaning up the droppings my boss has made, and if that makes me look good, then I'm doing my job!"

"Okay, gentlemen, you've told me that my nephew's nightmares, his fear, and everything else are not enough, so where do we go from here?"

"I hate to say this, Allen, but we hold our position, and we wait!" Sam said.

I looked at Dunbar, and he knew that wasn't going to happen.

"Here's some food for thought, Mr. Watkins. It's evident that you've walked into my space not knowing who I am because if you did, you wouldn't have said what you just did. I've built my reputation, and here's what I'm going to do for you! I'm not going to put a bullet in Mr. Simms's head, and I'm going to help you look good! When this is over, you'll owe me a favor or maybe two, and if you forget about this day or turn your back on me or Detective Dunbar, I'll drag you through a ten-acre field of broken glass. Are we straight on that?"

Sam looked at me and back at Dunbar and knew that I had just committed myself to helping him capture his boss's seat and help him build his career up. "You have my solemn promise, Allen," he swore with is hand stuck out for a handshake.

I refused it and stared back up to his eyesight. "Forget that, Sam. This ain't the country club area, and you're in my neighborhood now. Are we straight on this or not?"

"Straight," he replied; at that point, I shook his hand.

"Hi, Sam." Michelle walked in and stood next to me. "I see you've had the pleasure of meeting my fiancée's rough side of the coin." She had a wide smile on her face.

I didn't know that Sam and Michelle knew each other. Smiling, Sam said, "Michelle and I had lunch to talk about the girls on the list, and I see you all keep the 'favor' standard in the family because I owe her one too."

"Well, before I go, I guess the only thing I can say is be careful how you deal with Mr. Simms because his power and influence is building rapidly and if he . . ."

"Excuse me, when we get his ass behind bars, it's going to be media frenzy, and his attorney is going to find any reason possible to tear this case down. So any mistakes you make today will be the reason he'll have the possibility of walking as a free man."

"Allen, but don't mess this up!"

"Please let me show you to the door, Mr. Future DA, because this conversation that never happened is over."

Dunbar gave me that "I'll get back with you later" look before I closed the door behind them.

The way I saw it, if it were not for Darius, this case wouldn't be a case. Dunbar and Sam were forming an alliance to build their futures, and like some good white folks, they couldn't do it without some help from a brother. I wasn't mad at them, but they left knowing that it wouldn't come free!

"Baby, are you okay?" Michelle asked.

I walked up to her and wrapped my arms around her waist. "No, I'm not, but I'm willing to maintain my sanity for you!"

"So what do we do now?" she asked.

"I need an uncut copy of the footage that Channel 10 news shot the day of Hope's murder."

"The one that showed Darius being carried out of the house?" she asked.

"Michelle, that's what they wanted the public to see. I want everything!"

She still didn't understand and was curious about why I would want to see that footage.

"Aunt Vera was worried about why Hope didn't show up for church and wasn't answering the phone, so she went over there. From the time the police were called, the news station was on the scene and most of the Mt. Zion Hill Church was there, except who, Michelle?"

"Donald," she whispered.

I went on. "He wouldn't even come after seeing his own son on a live breaking news coverage being carried out of the house with blood covering him from head to toe, but he showed up at the courthouse to claim him."

"I'll call Peterson and have him call in one of his favors at the station," Michelle stated.

Michelle left the room briefly and called Peterson. "Pete said that he would have someone run over to the station and pick up a copy within the hour, and you know he asked why!"

"What did you tell him?"

"I told him that I was the one requesting the footage, not you."

"Question? How would a mother put her child to bed?" I asked her.

"What?"

"Come on Michelle, clotheswise."

"At least in some pajamas, a T-shirt or something," she insisted.

"What did Darius have on?"

"A towel was wrapped around him. Maybe the medics took or cut his clothes off to see if he was bleeding too."

"Aunt Vera will know how Hope dressed him for bed, and if she tells me Hope normally dressed him and I find out he was just in his underwear, then somebody came in contact with him before they left that house. If Darius was up or woke up and saw whoever it was, they might have tried to put him back to bed and stained his clothes or something."

"Trey, if that were the case, the police would have found some kind of trace in Darius's room."

"Well, we'll see what Aunt Vera has to say about this." I wasn't hit over the head for nothing.

It was after midnight when I walked into the *Herald,* and Pete was running around like a chicken with its head cut off. That was up my alley! If I was correct, he had already reviewed the footage and wanted more information from me. I really didn't have to guess where the tape was after seeing the VCR sitting on top of his TV.

I just walked in his office, pushed play, and there it was. The cameraman had a good standard relationship with the police and fire departments when it came to recording scenes of any sort. Not only would they focus on the main story, but they would take good angle shots of the crowd from the time they got there until the time they wrapped things up. The cameraman that shot this footage rolled up on the essence with two pistols drawn and shooting footage way before the news van ever pulled up. *This dude is good!* They had a lot of footage on Aunt Vera repeatedly asking about Darius and wanting to know if he was all right. The police wouldn't tell her anything at first, but seeing that she was about to blow, they had Darius carried away by a medic.

Just as I suspected, no clothes! I backed the footage up and paused it at the best shot I could get, and it brought tears to my eyes to see Darius covered in so much blood, desperately trying to reach out to Aunt Vera. I backed the footage up all the way to the start of the shooting; it was 12:32 a.m. I fast-forwarded it to where Darius was being brought out, and it read 1:18 a.m. I backed it up again to check the arrival time of the ambulance, and it read 12:37 a.m. They had thirty minutes to deal with Darius before they brought him out. I grabbed the phone and called Dunbar at home. He muttered "yeah" when he answered.

"Dunbar, please tell me you were in the house prior to the medics bringing Darius out."

"Yeah, why?"

"What did he have on, Dunbar?"

"His damned underwear, Allen, so what's up?"

"You have kids, Dunbar?"

"What the hell does that have to do with the case, dude?"

"Do you or not?" He replied that he had a two-year-old.

"Do you put the kid to sleep or does your wife?"

"My wife. Why?"

"Women around the world don't change, Dunbar. Walk into your child's room, and look at your child. Tell me what was missing when you found Darius. The coroner ruled her death around eleven or midnight, Dunbar. If your child was asleep like Darius was, think about it, and you'll find out what was missing. I'm at the *Herald*." I hung up, knowing I had him thinking.

"So what the hell was missing, Allen?" Pete asked as he started the tape from the beginning.

"Darius didn't have on his sleeping clothes, Pete!"

"What did Dunbar say?"

"Just his underwear," I replied. We got quiet for about five minutes as the footage rolled on. "Pete, if Darius woke up because of an argument that was going on and walked in on a panicking person, would the person put Darius back in the bed?"

"I would," he replied.

"Okay, what if the argument didn't wake him up? What if it was the noise of somebody busting up the coffee table to make it look like Hope had hit her head?"

"I would still put him back to bed," Pete said.

That could mean the person could have gotten some blood on Darius's pajamas and took them off him.

"Stop the tape! Stop it!" I shouted as I grabbed the remote from his hand. I rewound the tape back to when Darius was being placed in the ambulance, and as soon as the back door was closed, I saw her! I got up on the television and pointed to her. I was more than disgusted!

"Who is she, Allen?" asked Pete.

Dunbar walked through the door and up to the TV for a closer look.

"Her name is Katrina Bible! She was found dead in the Motel 9, overdosed on heroin," Dunbar told Pete. "I should have followed up that Saturday before Hope's funeral." Dunbar continued to stare at her, turned to get the remote out of my hand, and rewound the footage back to Darius.

"No clothes," he said as he looked at me with a stiff look.

"If Kat didn't do it, she knew about it, and if she wasn't in the house, she knew who was there. She also knew Darius was alone in the house, and that maternal instinct of hers kicked in. As soon as the ambulance drove away with Darius, she left too."

"If I round up all of Donald's ex-girls, especially the one we talked to last night, he'll know that we're getting closer to him," Dunbar said.

"Listen, Dunbar. I've thought long and hard about this, and the only person that can make me drop the notion exhuming Hope's body is my aunt Vera. If she tells me that Hope always dressed Darius for bed, I'm trusting that Darius is right about his blanket or at least the possibility that I might not have noticed it."

"Come on, Allen. You said that you stood over her at the funeral, and I'm not color blind but all that purple, yellow, and blue? What are you saying?"

"Okay, Dunbar, look at the picture before you close the door on this. Let's say I would have arrived at my parents' house at the same time as whoever hit me in the head."

"We would have what that person came back to a murder scene to get, right? Dunbar, if your little boy—"

"Girl," he corrected. I smiled and kept on. "Okay, if your little girl couldn't find something dear to her, and I walked in the house with it, and she saw it, would she want it?"

"We would never get peace until she got it!" he replied.

"Then I'm trusting Darius. Whatever Hope took that belongs to him was dear, and I haven't gotten any peace, Dunbar! Every time he sees a picture and that damn blanket is in it, the only thing he keeps saying is 'Mama take it! Mama take it, Uncle Trey.'"

Pete was supporting my theory. "Allen has a valid point, Detective."

"Do you know where I'll be if nothing turns up in that casket, Allen?"

"All I know is where we'll all be if something is in the casket, Dunbar! I almost got killed the night before the funeral, and Hope was lying right next door to Donald all night. If it was him who hit me, he could make it back home without any problems. I'm putting my money on Darius!"

"Pete, talk to me." I was looking for his input on what I had just said.

"I'm placing my money on the kid as well. Donald had all night to stuff Hope's casket if he wanted to hide something, and who would have guessed of such a thing as exhuming a body to recover a murder weapon?"

"Come on, Dunbar. We're not dealing with a naive schoolboy but a very meticulous street thug that had survival on his mind no matter what."

The phone rang and Pete answered it on the second ring. "Peterson. Is everything all right?" He handed the phone to me. "It's Michelle." What was the look on his face?

"Baby, what's wrong?"

"Trey, Donald is leaving," she said through her crying.

"What do you mean he's leaving?"

"Trey, he's leaving Waco!" She didn't know where he was going, she said harshly, but she knew he was leaving. I didn't want to make her lash out at me, so I carefully asked her how she found out that Donald was leaving Waco.

"How else, Trey?"

"Darius?" I asked.

"He's right here with me and do you want to know what he's been saying for the past thirty minutes?"

I could hear Michelle telling Darius to come and sit on her lap to talk to Uncle Trey. When I heard his breathing on the phone, I knew he had had another dream.

"Hi, Darius. Talk to Uncle Trey, little man." I placed the call on the speaker phone so that Dunbar and Pete could hear him.

"Mama take it, Trey! She take it!"

"Where did she take it, Darius?"

"Mama take it, Trey!"

"No, nephew, tell Uncle Trey where Mama take it?" Suddenly we all heard the phone fall on the hard surface and heard Darius in the distance.

Michelle picked up the phone, crying and explained that Darius was repeatedly patting the bedroom floor as he continued to say that his mama took it.

"Baby, do you need me?" I asked as I took her off the speaker.

"Trey, Samantha's gone," she cried out.

"Michelle, she'll be back. Don't trip." I tried to sound reassuring.

"No, Trey. She told me that she loved me and that she was glad that I was happy. She said she likes you and then said that the bad man is leaving. I asked her what bad man. Then Darius walked in and woke me up. Trey, I don't want her to go."

I could hear a hollowness, an anguish in Michelle's voice as she cried.

"Michelle, listen to me, sweetheart. Do you know why she really stayed with you? Because you never left her side when it mattered. She knows that her mother is happy now, and now she can move on too. She knows that you will be okay. You never have to let her go in your heart, baby, but it would be so selfish to even ask her to remain away from a place we all want to be one day. Can you feel me, baby?"

"I love her so much, Trey. I need to visit her today and take some flowers."

"She knows you love her, Michelle. I'll bring some home with me, but I need to know that you're going to be okay, baby!"

"I am. Finish what you were doing, and you listen to my baby and to Darius. You understand?"

I assured her I understood clearly, and she told me that she loved me before ending the call.

"Okay, gentlemen. I'm back, and the tides have shifted. Dunbar, I need for you to trust me on this because I really can't explain it right now, but you have to please trust me!"

"I'm listening, dude!"

"Donald is leaving the city. When, where, or what time I don't know, but I need you to keep an eye on him because I want his ass in Waco when we raise that casket out of the ground."

Dunbar looked at me and back at Pete.

"Peterson, do you have a job for an ex-detective?" Dunbar asked with a stone look on his face.

"Son, if Chief Malone raises as much as an eyebrow toward you if we find nothing in that girl's casket, I promise you he will be very sorry."

Dunbar reached for the phone and started punching in his fate. "Let's get this situation behind us and Simms in a six-by-nine box," he stated. "Captain Miles, Dunbar speaking, sir. I need a twenty-four-hour surveillance approved on a Donald Simms, a murder suspect that is about to skip town on me, and I need him to be in this city or where I can put my hands on him after I get the results run on a murder weapon."

"Detective, are we speaking about the Reverend Donald Simms?"

"Yes, sir, we are!"

"Listen here, Detective, the chief had to kiss Reverend Simms's attorney's ass for that stunt you pulled at his home. They wanted to sue the city behind that. Now you're talking about messing with this man again? What evidence do you have, and it better be sound, Detective!"

"Sir, I strongly believe that Donald Simms placed the murder weapon on the inside of Hope Allen's casket the night prior to her funeral, sir."

"It's almost three in the morning, and you want me to approve a twenty-four-hour tag on an influential figure in this city based on what you believe, Detective? You've got to be losing your mind!"

"Okay, you listen and you listen close because I'm only going to say this one time," Dunbar said with sure conviction. "You are going to approve this surveillance, and if you don't, I'll personally make sure that you will be checking parking meters downtown before the end of the month! I want to know what time Simms takes his first piss, what hand he wiped his butt with until my lab work is completed, and if you don't approve this, I'm making a wake-up call with the same attitude I got right now. So what's it going to be, Officer Miles?"

"I don't know who the hell you think you are talking to, Detective, but I'm ordering you back here to this department at once, and if you are not here within the next hour, I'm filing insubordination charges on you. Do I make myself clear, Detective?"

"Have it your way, Miles. When you write the proper paperwork, please get the spelling of my name right. Roll that paperwork up real tight because I would hate for you to get a paper burn while you are shoving it!"

Dunbar hung up the phone and turned to Pete, pushed the phone closer to Pete, and told him to punch in his boss's home number. Pete reached for his rolodex, found the chief's number, and punched them in.

"Chief Griffin, it's early and it can't wait! I've followed procedures and can't get what I need, sir. I need for you to approve a twenty-four-hour surveillance on Donald Simms because he's about to leave the city, and I need to know exactly where he is when I get the results back on my evidence, sir."

"Are you out of your mind calling my house at this time of the morning with this crap, Detective?"

"Since you asked, sir, I am out of my mind, and I really hope you just go ahead and approve the tag on the suspect, sir. PLEASE!"

"I want your ass in my office at 7:00 a.m. sharp, Detective, and your request is denied!" Pete snatched the phone out of Dunbar's hand and went far left field with Chief Griffin.

"Grif, this is Peterson. I've sat here and watched you move up in the ranks to your position, and I've even glorified your ass in my paper. This detective is on the edge of solving this Allen case, and your bureaucratic bull is in the kid's way! You're either going to give the boy what he needs, or I'm calling a friend in from the Texas Rangers' office here in Waco to do your job for you! I assure you, Ranger Fields won't tell me no, and as soon as Detective Dunbar's results come back in and Simms is placed behind bars, I'm writing a front-page run on you and your sorry ass officers that stood in this man's way. On top of that, Trey Allen and his soon to be wife, Michelle Evans, you know the name don't you, Grif? Well they will be doing a front-page run until they reach a climax on the way you allowed the deaths of some black known prostitutes to be signed off as suicides when you knew they were murdered."

Peterson had me fascinated, but he wasn't finished. "So you can save yourself some more trouble surrounding the African-American community! Now you give this detective what he needs right this damned minute! And for the record, since we both know that Donald Simms is well-known in quite a few states, all my alliances in the Associated Press will know about Simms as a killer and how courageous and dedicated Detective Dunbar was despite his adversaries in his own damn department. I wouldn't blame him for leaving your squad once this case is closed! So does the kid get what he needs, or do we have to call elsewhere, Griffin?" Pete's tone sounded as if the matter was final.

"He's got until his results come back, and I want to see him in my office before my coffee gets cold Monday morning," Chief Griffin said just before he hung up the phone.

"You got your tag, son, and I would advise you to wait until daybreak before you call up any judge on an order to exhume your sister."

"Come on, Pete, you have to let your nuts hang real low, baby," I said with a taste of humor.

"Yeah, how low do yours hang?" he asked.

"Hell you're the one with the rolodex, big daddy," I said as I pushed the rolodex in front of him.

"Not until daybreak, boys. I'm no fool!"

I grabbed the phone and called up Gwendolyn. "This better be important," she said with a groggy bite!

"I wouldn't be calling if it wasn't, Gwen."

"Is something wrong with Michelle?" she asked in a panic.

"No, ma'am, but after we're done, I'd like for you to call her. I know any little thing is important to you when it comes to her and I highly respect that, Gwen!"

"So what's that important, Trey, at this time of the morning?"

"Samantha, Gwen. She told Michelle that Donald Simms is leaving town, and Darius is wide awake about that blanket being in Hope's possession."

"If Samantha said he's leaving, you better take her word for it, and I'm telling you this is based on what we discussed. I understand you, man!"

"That's why I'm on the phone with you, Gwen. Detective Dunbar has put his career on the line for me, Darius, and Hope because of something you and I both understand. He just got off the phone with the chief about getting a twenty-four-hour watch on Donald and things got real ugly, but there was no backing down until he got it. What I need from you right now is your influence. I need a judge to issue Dunbar an order to exhume Hope so that we can get what Darius says is in there right now."

"My niece is happy you came into her life and loves you. When she told me that she won't go through with this wedding until this investigation is complete, I was sad, so I'll do anything to see her happy, Trey! You and Dunbar get someone out to her grave site with the equipment ready, and I'll have your court order delivered to you at the site within the hour."

"Thank you, Gwen." When I hung up, Dunbar was so anxious, he couldn't wait for me to tell him if we had the order or not.

"She wants us down at the grave with the equipment ready, and she'll have the order brought to us with the hour."

"Yes!" Dunbar shouted and held his hand up for a high five.

"Hey!" Pete shouted, "Get the hell out of my office. I'm trying to run a newspaper company, not some hangout for knuckleheads, and I'm expecting your hands on the up-and-coming column, Mr. Allen."

"Yes, sir, boss," I said and couldn't help hugging him before I left.

Dunbar had to threaten the local funeral home owner before the man moved a finger on getting his men and equipment out to the gravesite because Dunbar didn't have the court order on hand. It was way after two hours when a familiar car pulled into the entrance of the cemetery. As the car got closer, I knew it wasn't a deputy's car. It was Gwendolyn. Was she there to tell us she couldn't get the order? Moments later, I saw the red-and-blue lights flashing from the tops of three patrol cars, followed by a sheriff department van.

"Please tell me you all didn't give up on me," Gwen said as she exited her car.

"Your Honor, we weren't leaving this cemetery without Hope, and since I've been told a wedding couldn't take place until this case was over, there was no way I would be the one to disappoint those involved."

"Sir, you might not know me, but my name is Judge Gwendolyn Evans. I have orders for you to start the backhoe, and turn the casket and the remains over to my deputies right now." She gave the owner the court order to raise Hope.

Raising Hope

Even before the brother operating the backhoe started to give the earth a warning, I felt I was at the crossroads with Hope, knowing that we both were at the right place yet feeling a sense of abandonment. I was blessed that she was with me in the middle of those roads.

The floodlights that hummed from the power of the diesel generator and the armed police manning the entrance to this place of the rested and of the unrest made me aware of the love for my sister. Though I couldn't see the thousands of souls rising from their graves to witness with questions, I could see Hope answering them with a simple statement, "Redemption for my son."

As soon as the bucket started to loosen the earth's grip on my sister, I felt Hope pushing her way up toward her redemption as well. For her, it was a long-awaited event, and knowing that her child was suffering did not sit well with her. I wanted to tell the machine operator to hurry, but it was evident that he was very nervous himself, so I empathized with the brother and his crew that stood ready to do the work the backhoe wasn't able to do.

"I can't know what you might be feeling right now, Trey, but knowing what I know about the power of God and knowing a fragment of what he will allow and what he won't, I believe that Hope pleaded with God not to let her child suffer behind a need of whatever is in that casket," Gwendolyn's voice was full of compassion.

"Michelle called me at home one morning about five and told me that a man would cut his wife and attempt to cut me too if I went to work that morning. I went despite the silly dream she had about her daughter. It was almost noon, but I decided to do one more custody hearing before breaking for lunch. The father was a drunk and very abusive to his wife. Though she appeared before me wanting to change her mind about the proceedings, all beat-up with physical bruises on her body from a previous beating, I rejected her plea to stop the proceedings. I denied the father rights to seeing his sons. I ordered that the boys be placed in protective custody. I heard the man say, 'Bitch, now look what you've done.' The man pushed his attorney to one side to get to his wife and stabbed her several times in her stomach before coming after me. I sat there in shock, remembering Michelle's now not-so-silly dream. So if Hope had anything to do with Darius's dreams, knowing that it was her only way to tell you who did this, I know she's hurt because of what her child had to go through to get this casket raised," Gwen said, rubbing her hand up and down my back to comfort me. "Nevertheless, God is good, Trey!"

"I think back as I replay Darius being carried out of the house in my mind, and all I can imagine is a hurt child growing up without his mother, and though God and I don't have that type of relationship, I pray that the little communication that I do will help me to be the best uncle I can be. I pray he won't be a bitter child," I told her before moving closer toward the hole in the ground.

As the bucket kept reaching in deeper and deeper, I was uncomfortable with the backhoe hitting the top of Hope's casket with its teeth as it continued to lift small portions of soil. One of the helpers pushed a long wooden probe down into the hole and tapped the top of the casket. "That's it," shouted the operator. One of the other men lowered a makeshift wooden ladder that was a mere piece of wood nailed together. I guess one of the brothers saw the confused look on my face and decided to answer the questions that rolled through my mind.

"We don't pull them out too often, so we kind of improvise. The little ladder that we use is lightweight but strong enough to hold us and won't damage the casket. It's going to take three of us to get the tie-downs ready just so we can get the lifting process ready. It won't be long now, maybe another fifteen minutes," he explained before walking to the edge of Hope's grave to wait his turn to go down the homemade ladder.

"How are you holding up, buddy?" Dunbar asked.

"I'm glad you're not coming to visit with me in jail. I want to apologize for my attitude back at Michelle's. I was way out of line with you, Dunbar, and I know you were trying to look out for me."

"I thought I was going to have to kick your ass for a minute there, dude," he said with a smile on his face.

"No comment, chump," I replied.

"Listen, Allen. I'm not opening the casket until I get it back to our storage, get it washed off, and ready for my CSI team to do what they do best. Though policy restricts unauthorized people from entering the compound, I don't think anybody would get in my way."

Seeing the men climb back out of Hope's grave one by one let me know that it was time to lift her casket out of the ground. "So how long will it take for them to run the evidence, Dunbar?"

"Fingerprints are all I'm going to need to arrest Donald, and they will run their computer graphics on the weapon, if it's in there, with the stored graphic shots of the wound and point of entry on her skull, so I say about two hours or so."

"I got Sam Watkins out of bed and left word for him to meet us there. However, he wants to line this up good enough. To keep Donald in jail without bond is going to depend on what he does from this point on, so he might stall Donald's arrest for another few hours."

"You've got to be joking, Dunbar!" I was so close to nailing this bastard, but I wanted it now.

"Look, Trey, if the dude can't go anywhere, he can't go anywhere! Sam will want every minor thing looked at before bringing this dude in, even the judge who arraigns him. He'll contact the chief to map out any plans that may be added to seal this thing because as soon as they arrest his ass, the media will be driving and flying in from every state, trying to cover this story. That means this city is going to be a mess," Dunbar explained.

I shook my head in agreement. "I didn't consider all of that, but it reminded me of when the Atlanta serial killer was finally caught. Atlanta's population went from four hundred thousand to over almost one million because of all the media. It was crazy!"

"Well, get ready for a portion of that because Donald's arrest is going to bring the big dogs out. You have to remember that he is well-known in many states."

"I need you to promise me something, Dunbar."

"Speak," he replied.

"Make sure he doesn't get a bond, because if he does, I swear on my nephew's life, I'll kill him!" At that point, I broke down. Tears began to pour from my eyelids as if I had never cried. Everything was coming out of me all at once.

"Don't you worry about that, buddy. I assure you that will never happen," Dunbar said as he patted my shoulder.

The engine revving up on the backhoe let Dunbar and me know that the casket was finally being lifted out. As the scoop rose higher, we saw it—Hope's coffin. Once the operator had Hope two or three feet above the surface, he swung the casket closer to the side where all soil was piled up to give his assistants the opportunity to remove the heavy buildup still attached to the casket. Once the casket was clean enough, Gwendolyn expressed her level of impatience.

"Gentlemen, I appreciate your extra effort, but I need to get where I'm going," she shouted. Hope's casket was swung around to a clearance and placed down on the ground. The worker unstrapped their slings and placed her casket into the van. We all left the cemetery.

With all the lights flashing from the tops of the officers' cars and from the front grills, you would have thought the president was coming through the city. We finally made it to the department's storage facility. Getting through security was a step-by-step process that every vehicle had to go through, and everybody had to sign in before entering. By the time Dunbar and I were allowed to enter, a man in some type of white suit was spraying down Hope's casket with a water hose. There were six other men and women in the same type of suits, waiting on the soil to be washed off and for the casket to be dried. Sam Watkins was on the scene, and from the look Dunbar had on his face, whoever Watkins was talking to kept a frown on Dunbar's face. I inquired about the man standing next to Watkins. Dunbar bitterly replied it was the chief.

"Well, I guess he's here to see if you're going to pan out on this, Detective. Are you nervous?"

"Hell no, in fact, I think he's here to kiss my ass, Trey."

"That's what I'm talking about, baby! But you gotta stand with an attitude, and when you get ready to walk over there, stay eye to eye with him and when you greet him, just say, 'What it do, playa?'"

We both started laughing to shake the jitters off as best we could. As soon as Hope's casket was dried, Dunbar and I joined Watkins, Chief Griffin, and Gwendolyn. I heard Dunbar take in and blow out two pockets of air to calm himself down.

"Chief, Sam," he said as he shook their hands. "Chief, this is Trey Allen, sir," Dunbar stated, introducing me.

"I already know the gentleman, and in fact, I have a newspaper clipping of you framed in my office from a story you covered on those three slain officers in Atlanta. I was proud to know a local helped out on the apprehension of the two men responsible," he mentioned, and he shook my hand.

"You ever thought about wearing a badge, young man?" he asked.

"Chief Griffin, I'm barely into hanging on to the little sanity I have left just being a journalist," I told him. They burst out in laughter.

Everybody got quiet as the casket top was raised. I took one step toward the casket to see for myself, and the chief placed a firm grip on my shoulder.

"Patience, son," he said in a calm voice.

One of the suited men looked our way and said, "We have a live one, people."

"What is that supposed to mean?" I quickly said as I looked at Dunbar for an explanation.

"The guy just informed us that the case is alive and breathing. Look," Dunbar said. I looked where he was pointing, and there it was, Darius's blanket, tightly wrapped-up in a clear plastic bag. I fell to my knees and cried out to God. Tears pouring, body trembling, I gave him all the praise. "Thank you, God! Thank you, God! Thank you, God."

Gwendolyn knelt down beside me and held me. She, too, cried.

"Trey," Dunbar called out my name. He stood next to one crime scene investigator who held up Hope's trophy. I stood back up and shouted through my sobbing if they found the clothing. It took the investigator about four seconds to hold up Darius's bloody T-shirt and then his pajama bottoms. I walked over to Dunbar and hugged him as if I would never see him again.

"Thank you for putting it all on the line, Dunbar. Thank you, man!"

"Nah, Trey. I owe you, Darius, Michelle, and your sister for keeping the evidence safe."

Dunbar and I watched as one of the CSI members started lifting bloody fingerprints off the trophy and storing them on little plastic devices.

"How long?" I asked the lab guy concerning the fingerprints.

He looked up at me and then back at Dunbar. He asked Dunbar if this was his case, and Dunbar confirmed it was. "An hour." He added, "The DA wants this perfect, and if I could, I would send the prints on, but I can't. One thing you can count on, though, is that you will have your killer." He held up seven sets of bloody prints.

Dunbar and I walked over to where Gwendolyn, Sam, and the chief were discussing Donald's arrest. I wanted to know how long Sam was going to wait.

"Trey, I'm trying to wait on those prints to come back with his name on them, and I have to wait to see what judge is going to pull his card. I don't want to bring Mr. Simms through any judge's court influence with a case this huge. Hell, once the media finds out, the courthouse will be a madhouse!"

"So I need this to go down as smoothly as possible. On top of all that, by two this afternoon, every reporter and journalist in the city will be hunting you down like a criminal, trying to get an exclusive interview, so you just might need to find a hiding place for you, Darius, and Michelle for a while."

"Yeah, I've thought about that," I said.

Gwendolyn raised an eyebrow at me. I looked at her only and cut off her thinking before she could even utter a word.

"Oh hell no, Gwen! Everyone in the city knows I'm engaged to your niece, in fact, I am going to pack us all up and leave town just as soon as the indictment papers are typed up."

"Well, Trey, I assure you that he will be in custody by noon," Sam stated. I looked at my watch and saw that it was fifteen minutes after five. I told Dunbar that I was headed out to be with my fiancée and nephew and informed him that we would be in church as soon as the doors opened this morning.

"Allen," said Sam cautiously.

"Calm down, Sam. My fiancée said this man was leaving, but not this city! So I've got to go listen to Reverend Simms live behind the lies of the pulpit one last time." Something inside made me hope they wouldn't arrest Donald during church service. I didn't care about him, but the people, did they deserve that?

"Gwendolyn, I'm getting married," I told her with joy as I hugged her.

"Yes, you are, Trey," she replied with an even bigger smile.

"Gentlemen, please have yourselves a blessed day because I'm free this morning, and I thank each of you! Dunbar, come take me to my casa, Detective."

My ride home with Dunbar was a speechless one, and when he pulled into the driveway, we looked at one another before I got out of his car.

"Go home to your own wife and child, Dunbar," I gently said as I closed the door. I never looked back. My life was peeping through the bedroom curtains, watching me walk toward the front door. As I entered the house, Michelle was just entering the living room with a most precious glow. All I could say to her was "It's over, baby." I closed the door behind me. She ran into my arms and cried.

"So what are you crying for, woman?"

"Because I'm happy, baby, plus, we can now have our lives back."

We didn't see Darius walking in the room and wiping his eyes. "Uncle Trey," he said with a soft, pitiful voice.

"Hey, little man." I reached down to pick him up only to be shaken by the words that came from his mouth. "Mama, Mama, Uncle Trey," he said as he pointed toward his bedroom. Michelle and I smiled at each other because we knew that he had dreamed about his mother.

"Yeah, nephew. Mama is okay now and so are you," I assured him and gently kissed his cheek. I handed him to Michelle because I needed to shower and get some sleep before starting the rest of my peaceful life.

When Michelle came into the room after getting Darius busy playing, I filled her in on everything that had happened. "They will come for Donald by noon, and I want to be there when they arrest him. They found Darius's blanket, the pajama set, and the trophy he used to kill her with."

"I'm going with you, Trey," Michelle said as she placed both of her hands on my face.

"I don't need Darius there, Michelle."

"Then Gwen will watch him because I'm going with you, and that's final!"

"She's probably still at the department holding facility, but do what you have to, just remember I don't want him there," I said in a firm tone. I showered and quickly fell asleep, not realizing how exhausted I really was. I was awakened by the smell of food and Michelle rubbing my chest.

As I began to refresh myself, I thought about where I could take Michelle and Darius. I knew I had to leave the state if I wanted any privacy.

When I walked out of the bathroom, I felt that something wasn't right. By the time I made it to the dining room, I realized Darius was missing, so I curiously asked where my boy was.

"Gwen and Mona are probably still fighting over him," she said.

I smiled, with a bit of relief, knowing that he was in good hands.

"As soon as we leave church, I want you to get back here and pack for about two weeks."

"Two weeks? Trey, where are we going for that amount of time?"

"By five this evening, this house, Aunt Vera's, Aunt Jean's, and my parents' house will be swarming with reporters from every state, and the shark-teethed journalists that don't know how to quit will be all around."

"You are right!"

"I don't know where we are going, and I can't get my hands on traveling funds until the morning, so we might end up at Gwen's until then. So what are you wearing, Mrs. Allen?"

"Since this is a special occasion, I thought I'd wear the dress I bought for you, and I hope you don't mind, but I went by Vera's to pick up a suit that would go real nice with my dress."

"So did you get me some accessories too, baby?" I teased.

"I have everything you'll need to bc the cleanest brother in the church." As I leaned over to kiss her lips, I whispered, "Good looking out for your man!"

Breakfast was short and sweet. Our drive to the church house offered bits and pieces of conversation as we realized the moment of truth was about to hit us squarely in the face. It was evident that Chief Griffin intensified security about a mile around the church in every direction. I purposely zigged in and out of the neighborhoods east, south, and west, traveling at least ten blocks away from the church and spotting unmarked cars and other law enforcement vehicles. I was so lucky, finding a parking spot that was close to the church due to all the visitors that normally show up on second Sunday each month. I double-parked and informed one of the police officers who I was and told him why I was there. He assured me that there wouldn't be a ticket on my car, or better yet, that it wouldn't be towed if I made sure to move it right after the arrest.

Michelle and I had reserved seats next to Aunt Vera and Aunt Jean, which were located in one of the best sections—center row, second pew, and a face-to-face stare at the pulpit. The choir was crunked, and the ministers from visiting churches were seated and waiting for Donald to enter. He was always fired up on a big entrance, and with the crowd as large as it was, it gave him even more reason to parade his grand entrance. He finally decided to grace the crowd with his presence and went straight to the pulpit to get situated. He did his usual opening with prayer as the choir continued to sing softly. Afterward, he did his usual welcoming of the guests.

"It is such a blessing to be here this morning, church. When I stand behind this pulpit and look amongst you, I'm reminded of what the Lord has done and how he continues to do great things for us. It makes me want to lift up holy hands to the Father and shout 'hallelujah!' When I see the faces of you, the church, I just want to praise his mighty name. Can I get an 'amen?'" Donald asking for replies from the audience lasted about two minutes, and he had to motion for a calm before the people would stop shouting how good God was and all the other glorious phrases they used.

"This morning, church, I want to talk to you about the great commission. If you have your Bibles, please turn with me to Matthew 28, verses 18-20. Please stand with me, church, for the reading of our Father's word, amen!"

The congregation responded with their amens before he continued.

"And it reads, 'And Jesus came and spoke unto them saying; all power is given unto me in Heaven and on earth. Go ye therefore and teach all the nations baptizing them in the name of the Father, the Son and the Holy Spirit. Teaching them to observe all things whatsoever I have commanded you, and lo; I am with you always, even unto the end of the world.' Amen!"

After hearing all the bull this man was feeding these innocent church-going people, I completely changed my mind about the arrest happening during the service. It took all I had to sit and listen as this wolf dressed in sheep's clothing continued to deceive. Still I felt sorry for all the people as I envisioned Dunbar walking Spoon's ass out of this church in handcuffs.

His sermon continued. "Church, when Jesus reached the age of thirty, he was baptized in the Jordan by John the Baptist. The Bible says that when he came up, I said when he came up out of the water, lo the heavens were opened up unto him, and the spirit of God descended like a dove and lighting upon him. A voice from heaven said, 'This is my beloved son, in whom I am well pleased.'"

Every time he paused, I looked at my watch, asking myself if it was time. Michelle leaned over and whispered, "Stop with the hard stare, Trey, and stop looking down at your watch." I guess I was being too obvious that something out of the ordinary was about to happen, but it was the wrong time and place for my actions.

His sermon continued about Jesus being led into the wilderness and not giving in to temptation, then being ministered to by the angels before he began his ministry of teaching, healing, consoling the crowds, and casting out demons. He just had to mention Judas Iscariot who betrayed Jesus for thirty pieces of silver and how the mob came to cuff him and lead him to Pontius Pilate.

"But for your ass, it will be Dunbar hauling you off to jail," I softly whispered. Michelle quickly pinched me on my thigh because she heard me. The sermon seemed to be never-ending as I continued to look back through the masses standing and praising every word Simms spoke. I thought to myself, *When will they stop the madness?*

As he attempted to keep the church stirred by speaking about Jesus being raised from the grave, we caught eyes for the fourth time, and I was hoping like hell he was reading my mind! *Yeah, you bastard. Hope was raised too! Amen!*

Donald's ability to make his voice rise and fall kept the congregation wound up, which made me wonder if the homeowners within a two-block radius could hear Mt. Zion Hill Baptist Church that morning.

When he began speaking about Jesus being seated at the right hand of the Father and how he was coming back for his church with all the glory, something came over me, and whatever the look on my face displayed, Michelle saw it and began to physically hold me down as I glared at this fool through the seams of people jumping up and down. I know he felt everything I was feeling because he did all he could not to draw attention to the fact that he kept staring back and forth at me through the remainder of his sermon.

"Church, our commission is to go out into the world, preaching the Gospel from city to city, state to state, and country to country. Jesus was our example, and we as followers of Christ must do as he did while he walked upon this earth. All of the prophets did it, Paul made three tours around Decapolis. It is our duty, our responsibility as ministers to spread the word wherever he chooses to send us. Therefore church, sad as it may be, I have something I must talk to you about this morning, and I know this is what the Lord wants me to do. I've been moved to preach in Los Angeles, California, and I have accepted my calling."

It was sickening listening to all the pleadings of the people, begging him not to go, telling him how much they needed the good reverend here. Such sadness came from these people's hearts.

Please come on, Dunbar, and end this mess, I closed my eyes and humbly asked. I felt Michelle's hand on my thigh as a plainclothes detective stood in the doorway at the back of the church, blocking where the choir usually marched through. This made me look around to see Dunbar and two other plainclothes detectives standing behind him. I remained seated and poised as Dunbar walked up to the pulpit and told him, "You can come down from there with some dignity, or I can handle your sorry ass the way I really want to. You have three seconds to turn around and put your hands behind your back!" Donald and I looked at each other for a split second in slow motion. He looked back at Dunbar, took a deep breath, and turned around to be handcuffed.

All hell broke loose. The people were on their feet, in complete disbelief, asking what was going on. What had he done so wrong that would make them come into the house of worship to arrest him in front of his congregation? As they started to walk him out, Dunbar looked over at me and winked to let me know it was truly over! I knew that I had to leave right behind Dunbar, with Aunt Vera, Aunt Jean, and Michelle closely following me, without making a scene. It was only a matter of time before the frenzy began, and I had to tell them about everything before the media came swarming down on them.

THE CALM

As soon as I left the church grounds, I explained everything to Aunt Vera and Aunt Jean and warned them of what life was going to be like within the next few hours. They were pretty shook-up about what had just happened in their place of worship, and more than anything, they were trippin' because I hadn't been keeping them abreast of the ongoing investigation concerning Spoon. With all the fussing they were doing, they were not understanding that they had limited time to prepare for the storm surge that was about to hit the city. I left them sitting in the car when I pulled up at Aunt Vera's house.

I picked up the phone and called Pete. Michelle had already told Pete that we were leaving, but I needed to know that he had a photographer on this. "Pete, please tell me that you have somebody down at the station getting my front-page shots!"

"Who am I?" he asked.

"Sorry for asking, Pete, and I'm sorry we have to work over the phone, but I need to shield my crew."

He had told Michelle that he wanted me to work from an undisclosed location, but I thought that was a joke! When I thought about the reporters from the Houston and Dallas area coming into town expecting some state priority love that I knew I owed only to my Atlanta-based newspaper, I made it clear very quickly that the door was closed to anyone else. According to Peterson, Atlanta was grateful for bringing them straight to the door, and they were sending some guy named

Carl Finken or something like that. I laughed when I heard Carl's name. That was a real joke. He was too scared to take on the color barrier issue with Atlanta's white and black proms.

"I hope you are going to pull this off, Allen!"

"Pete, I have the assistant DA giving a play-by-play before it hits the courtroom. I've got Dunbar, a department sketch artist, and you."

"So what's on your agenda first?" Pete asked.

"Let me pack up, get Michelle and Darius over to Gwen's, and I'll be headed down to the police department. Dunbar is giving me access to listen in on the interrogation and providing me with a copy of that meeting. He won't start until Simms has been arraigned, so that will give me some time to get my family squared away. I'll give you exclusive knowledge on his relationship with Hope and how he evaded prosecution from federal charges. So don't worry." Then, with an attitude, I said, "Who am I?"

"Only my best journalist and the rocket fuel I've needed around this place for quite some time! Get situated, and get your ass down to the station before I fire you on the first day!"

Michelle remained lip locked as Aunt Vera and Aunt Jean continued to carry on about Spoon, and with the phone ringing with more nosy church members, I was quickly after my clothes and luggage.

"Baby, please get me out of here. I didn't realize your aunts could go like that, and Jean had the nerve to tell me that I should have called one of them to tell them about the arrest beforehand."

"Welcome to the family, baby," I said with a sarcastic laugh. I kissed her lips to help ease her. "Now don't just stand there looking beautiful, woman. Grab that bag, and let's get out of this joint! Channel 10 has first bids on everything, and I am sure they are about ready to air live, so we don't have much of a head start."

"You are cute when you are amped up like this, baby," she told me in a flirtatious way.

"Michelle, you're flirting."

"I am."

I had to bust in on my aunt's so-called conference call. Aunt Jean was in the kitchen, and Aunt Vera was in the living room, talking to who knows who, and after telling them the final time to shut down the house and leave, both of them just waved me off. So I did the only thing I could do. I left them babbling.

"I'll bet you by Tuesday, your aunts will be on *Good Morning Waco* and any other news show that will have them."

"So what are you trying to say about my family, woman?"

"The media won't have a chance," she said, laughing. "They will invite them in to eat and give them more than they ever bargained for!"

"Girl, if you weren't my fiancée I would put you out of my car—talking about my people like that."

She just lay over on my shoulder and laughed until tears flowed from her eyes.

It was about two hours before I made it to the police department, and as I walked into the lobby, I was face-to-face with the desk sergeant who was normally in uniform and on the other side of the desk. He stuck his hand out for a shake and said I had done good work. "If you ever need me for anything, just ask." He whistled at the officer maintaining the desk to show me to Dunbar's desk right away.

I called him sergeant and told him thanks.

"That's Lieutenant, young man," he said with a smile on his face as he walked out of the station.

I walked up on Dunbar while he was on the phone. Looking down on his cluttered desk, I saw a picture of his wife and daughter. I couldn't help but smile because the white boy had good taste.

"Tom, this is Allen, take him to the lookout. Give me a minute, and I will be right there," he directed. He covered the phone and pointed at his wife to let me know that's who was on the other end.

I followed the officer until he opened a door and ushered me in and informed me there was coffee and water if I wanted it and a phone to call out if I needed. The only thing that caught my eye was Spoon sitting on the other side of the two-way window. He sat there dressed in a two-piece orange jail-issued uniform.

I walked up to the window and stared as hard as I could. He could sense my presence, I was sure, and then he slowly raised his head and looked toward the window as if the two-way never existed. I had an urge to move two steps to my right just to see if he was staring straight through the window. Then he started to nod his head up and down as though he acknowledged my presence. It was just me and him, and the only thing that separated us was the window. I looked up at the monitors hanging from all four corners and back at the TV, recording every square inch of that room.

I thumped the glass lightly to get his attention, and he smiled this smirk-like grin as he continued to slowly bob his head up and down.

Then he spoke. "Negro, I should have killed your ass when I had the chance!" The grimace look on his face only confirmed that he knew I was there.

I thumped the window twice more, making him even more irate. Squirming in his chair, he yelled out again, looking directly at the window. "You ain't shit, schoolboy! I shoulda killed your nigga ass!" He snatched at the handcuffs and chains that had him pinned to a bolted table. Two police officers rushed in on him to calm him down, and as he sat down slowly, he made a final remark. "You gotta keep it pimpin', baby," he said as he winked at me.

Dunbar walked into the interrogation room and sat in a chair on the other side of Spoon. "Mr. Simms, though you already know my name, I have to officially state my full name for the record because this conversation is being recorded." As soon as he heard Dunbar mention that the meeting was being recorded, his attention quickly came back to me in amazement. He knew his actions prior to Dunbar entering had also been recorded. As he stared with an ill look on his face through squinted eyes, I wanted so badly to tap on the glass again but I couldn't because Chief Griffin and Sam were on their way through the door. So the only thing I had to say back to him was "You gotta keep it pimpin', baby!"

Sam, the chief, and I shook hands, and all listened very quietly. "My name is Detective Tim Dunbar of the Waco Police Department, and the time of day is 3:41 p.m., Sunday, the seventeenth of July, 1981. Mr. Simms would you please state your full name, sir?"

"Donald Wayne Simms."

"Have you been read your rights, Mr. Simms?"

He responded yes.

"Then you understand that anything you say, can and will be used against you in a court of law?"

"Yeah, I understand," Spoon replied as he looked back toward me and again back toward Dunbar. "Mr. Simms, you have volunteered to give this interview without your attorney present, is that correct?" Again he replied yes. Dunbar continued, "Mr. Simms, on or about the hour of 10:00 p.m., Saturday, June 10, did you visit Hope Alexandria Allen at her home?"

"Yes!"

"Did you kill Ms. Hope Alexandria Allen, Mr. Simms?"

Spoon looked my way and replied, "It was an accident."

Dunbar repeated the question, "Mr. Simms, did you kill Ms. Hope Alexandria Allen, sir?"

"Yes!" This time the cockiness had left.

"For the record would you please tell me exactly what happened the night of the murder?"

You could hear a pin drop because everyone was eager to hear his confession.

"Yeah, she asked me to stop by, said she had something she wanted to tell me. For two years I had been waiting on her to own up about Darius being my son. I asked her to give me a little time because I was tied up on another matter. She told me that if I couldn't come right then to just forget it!"

"What other matter was that, Mr. Simms?"

"I was helping a friend out with some money, and I had her in the car with me. I didn't want to take her over to Hope's with me."

"Did you end up taking this friend to Hope's anyway?"

"I didn't have a choice. I had to show up right then or not at all!"

Dunbar asked him to state his friend's name for the record and Spoon replied that it was Kat.

Dunbar then asked him to state her full name, and he responded, "Katrina Bible."

"So did Katrina Bible go into Hope's house with you?"

"No, she sat in the car."

"At no time did she go into the house. Is that correct?"

"Yes."

"Mr. Simms, when you went into the house, what happened?"

Spoon started squirming and took a deep breath. "She had just put Darius to sleep, and she told me it was too late for me to see him. She used him to get me over there because she had gotten wind that I was giving Katrina and a few more females money to fix with—"

Dunbar interrupted him by asking, "When you say 'fix' what do you mean?"

"To score some dope—heroin, man! She asked me about it, and I told her the truth. Then she just went off on me, telling me how disrespectful I was to the church and how I was an embarrassment to her and Darius. Then she started punching and swinging at me, hitting me in the face, ribs, and back with some heavy blows. The woman was literally starting to kick my ass, and I struck back, man!" He stated as tears ran down his face.

"I just reacted, Detective. She kept hitting me and hitting me. I begged her to stop. I put my hand on the closest thing to me and swung. Then she just fell on the floor. I didn't know exactly where I had hit her until I saw the blood starting to run down the side of her face."

He stopped for a few seconds and dropped his head. "I did everything I could to wake her up, and when I saw that she wasn't breathing anymore, I just panicked, man!"

Dunbar took a very quick glance toward the window. "So what did you do next?"

"I ran out to the car and got some of Katrina's dope, a syringe, and went back into the house. I gave her a shot of heroin and broke the table to make it look like an accident."

"Did Darius witness your hitting Hope or shooting her with dope?"

"No, man, none of that! He woke up before I was ready to leave the house. She was just lying there bleeding, man. I couldn't let him see her like that so I took him back to his room."

"What did you do next, Mr. Simms?"

"He had blood on his clothes." Dunbar asked him who had blood on their clothes. "Darius". I got blood on Darius's clothes. I took his clothes off and wrapped them up in a blanket along with the trophy that I hit Hope with."

"So what did you do next, Mr. Simms?"

"I couldn't take the stuff back to the car, so I put everything under the seat of the riding lawn mower."

At that moment I knew Dunbar must be saying the same thing in his mind that I was when he gave up his hiding place.

"Then what?"

"I left her house, dropped Katrina off at her motel room, and went to one of my old street buddies to clean up."

"At what point did you return to Hope's house to get the trophy, clothes, and blanket?"

Spoon looked back over toward the two-way window and frowned. "The night before her funeral!"

"When did you put the items in Hope's casket, Mr. Simms?"

"About two hours after I made it back to my house that night."

"Is there anything else you would like to say before we end this conversation, Mr. Simms?"

I quickly grabbed a pen and pad from the table by the window and scribble a note.

I folded the paper and asked one of the officers standing on the outside of the interrogation room to give the note to Mr. Simms. The officer entered the room and whispered into Dunbar's ear as he gave Dunbar the note. Dunbar unfolded the note, read it, folded it back up, and slid it to Spoon. Spoon slowly unfolded the note and read it.

"Got to keep it pimpin', baby, and if you don't say it, you're a street hoe yourself!" Spoon cracked a smirk. "Yeah, there's something I'd like to say. Hope was a certified, registered martial arts fighter. You know that, so I was defending myself." His eyes locked on the window, and he winked at me.

Four months later

Whether or not Spoon knew what he was doing, Sam made it understood that he wanted a jury trial and nothing less. The only offer that Sam placed on the table for Spoon was a life sentence. Sam didn't give a damn about his willingness to cooperate with him or Dunbar in the beginning. Three months went by, and the only thing that was changing for him was the jury selection. Spoon sat with his attorneys the prior weekend and saw no way out or past that life sentence. He had been around Waco too long to know that taking a chance with a jury might have meant receiving a sentence far beyond the years he would have to do on a life sentence.

The following Monday, Sam allowed Spoon to cop out for a life sentence, and the court accepted his agreement. When Sam told me about the plea agreement, I was concerned that the length of time Spoon was going to have could be reduced a few years down the road, perhaps for good behavior on his part, but Sam assured me that he had to serve twenty-five calendar years before he would be eligible to see the parole board. And even then, Sam explained, after they reviewed the footage of Spoon ranting on about how he should have killed me when he had the chance, they would surely deny his parole request for at least another ten years. The fact that he would be almost sixty-six when that time came around gave me pure joy.

I didn't see Spoon until Tuesday when he appeared in court, a far cry from the man who wore tailored suits, spit-shined shoes, and a modeled, prestigious look. His hair was wild, and it looked more like a rat's nest. He shuffled in the courtroom behind several other detainees, shackled at his ankles and handcuffed at his waist with a chain. It was evident that he was a broken spirit, and from the looks of him, he had lost twenty or so pounds. His face was sunken in, resembling that of a skeleton, and his arms were tiny, almost like those of a child. He reminded me of a stage IV cancer patient—frail, ashy, and defeated. Steve Collins, who was assigned to take all my photos for the column, was the only photographer allowed in Judge Macy's courtroom, courtesy of Gwendolyn.

As Spoon entered, his gracing-the-camera days were over, and he found no need to front any longer. He was worn-out, almost despondent. Giving that open confession sealed his fate and left him no chance of any appeal of any sort. It was truly over for him.

As soon as Steve's camera started shooting, Spoon started scanning the courtroom. He knew I was somewhere in the room, and he kept searching until he found me. We danced the stare-down. For the benefit of closure, Sam asked the judge if he would open his proceedings with Spoon's plea first, and the judge nodded his head in agreement. I raised my index finger to him as a *thank you*, and the judge called Spoon before his bench.

"Mr. Watkins, is the state ready this morning?" the judge asked.

"Yes, sir, Your Honor, we are." Sam handed the bailiff Spoon's file, and in turn, the bailiff handed the file to the judge.

"In the State of Texas, County of McLennan comes Donald Wayne Simms. Is that correct sir?" he asked Sam.

"Yes, Your Honor. That is correct," Sam replied.

I sat there, listening to all the normal statements. I heard Spoon's weak voice again admit to his guilt. I heard the judge's voice and the prosecutor's, but the only words that I actually remembered were those of the judge—his sweet, liberating words.

"Mr. Donald Wayne Simms, I hereby sentence you to life in prison and remand you to the custody of the Texas Department of Corrections until the term of that sentence is served."

The gavel hitting against the bench jolted Spoon back from whatever daze he was in, and he stood there looking at the judge with a loss of self. "Bailiff, remove this prisoner from my courtroom at once," the judge ordered as Spoon shuffled his way behind the doors. I wanted so badly to tell him to "Keep it pimpin'," but he seemed wounded enough.

Michelle and I stood up to leave as Spoon marched past us. His last gesture to me, a wink from his squinted eyes, was clearly filled with hate.

As soon as I left the courthouse that day, I went to the *Herald* to write my final column on Spoon. Putting his story on paper was closure for me. It allowed me to go on with my life. Michelle and I were married a month later and made plans to stay in Waco until Darius graduated from high school.

As for Hope, she was raised for Darius's sake. Then she was laid to rest in peace, knowing that I had not let her down and that Darius would be just fine.

A Shift in My World

Johnny A. McDowell

Coming Spring 2012

A Shift in My World

Caught between a life of loyalty and love, Catalina finds herself forced
to stand by the side of a man who could cost her her very life. This
soft-spoken Honduras princess quickly has to decide whether to live
under the cartel's rule or stand against it. Meanwhile, Stephon is thrown
into adulthood by the one man he trusted, Uncle James, who is the leader
of a secret brotherhood that lives by the motto "Use or be used!" Two
worlds collide when Stephon and Catalina meet and begin a love affair
that is not only forbidden but deadly. In an attempt to free her people
from oppression, she joins forces with Stephon who learns he must bring
down the one man who has taught him everything he knows.

For more information, please contact the author at thol1962@gmail.com.